"You're the most beautiful woman I've ever known, Tish,"

Kern murmured huskily. "I want you like something—clawing inside of me. I always have."

He was silent, but when she reached up with trembling hands he simply clasped them in an iron-fast hold, and then let her go. The sheet was smoothed to her breasts; he leaned over to press a tantalizingly sweet kiss on her forehead. A brother's kiss. Shocked sapphire eyes watched him stand erect.

"No, Tish, not tonight," he murmured. "I don't want Dutch courage between us. It matters too much—not for me, but for you."

Dear Reader:

As the months go by, we continue to receive word from you that SECOND CHANCE AT LOVE romances are providing you with the kind of romantic entertainment you're looking for. In your letters you've voiced enthusiastic support for SECOND CHANCE AT LOVE, you've shared your thoughts on how personally meaningful the books are, and you've suggested ideas and changes for future books. Although we can't always reply to your letters as quickly as we'd like, please be assured that we appreciate your comments. Your thoughts are all-important to us!

We're glad many of you have come to associate SECOND CHANCE AT LOVE books with our butterfly trademark. We think the butterfly is a perfect symbol of the reaffirmation of life and thrilling new love that SECOND CHANCE AT LOVE heroines and heroes find together in each story. We hope you keep asking for the ''butterfly books,'' and that, when you buy one—whether by a favorite author or a talented new writer—you're sure of a good read. You can trust all SECOND CHANCE AT LOVE books to live up to the high standards of romantic fiction you've come to expect.

So happy reading, and keep your letters coming!

With warm wishes,

Ellen Edwards

Ellen Edwards
SECOND CHANCE AT LOVE
The Berkley/Jove Publishing Group
200 Madison Avenue
New York, NY 10016

Second Chance at Love®

MAN FROM TENNESSEE
JEANNE GRANT

SECOND CHANCE AT LOVE
BOOK

MAN FROM TENNESSEE

First edition published May 1983

First printing

"Second Chance at Love" and the butterfly emblem are trademarks be-
longing to Jove Publications, Inc.

Printed in the United States of America

Second Chance at Love books are published by
The Berkley/Jove Publishing Group
200 Madison Avenue, New York, NY 10016

1

TRISHA HADN'T NOTICED when the rolling emerald hills of Kentucky had become the Tennessee mountains. Her attention was on the hairpin-curved road. Then suddenly she remembered the crisp spring air and the sweet scents of pine and wildflowers in bloom. And the fleeting mists that drifted between the mountain peaks. She recalled the peace, privacy, and silence that were the gift of the mountains. Silently she wished she hadn't remembered.

"Patricia!"

Trisha glanced swiftly at her mother-in-law. "Oh, you're awake. Are you feeling better, darling?"

"I would probably feel perfectly fine if I thought I could get your attention for two and a half seconds," Julia said petulantly. "You've been as quiet as a tomb for two days. Obviously you're still irritated with me."

For a few seconds Trisha's sapphire eyes met Julia's. A strong, independent spirit shone clearly in her mother-in-law's steel-blue eyes. Julia was a matriarch from a bygone era who could and would put anyone in his place, given the opportunity. But she didn't have to use

1

her formidable will against Trisha and they both knew
it.

"There was no one else I could ask, Patricia. Besides,
it isn't as if I ever asked much of you."

"I'm not arguing with you, darling," Trisha said wearily. "We're nearly there, so please just . . . let it be."

"You couldn't possibly be afraid to see Kern again,
could you?"

Trisha's fingers tensed on the wheel.

"The last time he saw you, you were a waif. And
now? Well, breeding will out, I've always said. You've
got aristocrat in your bones—"

"Thank you." Trisha interrupted dryly. "But what that
has to do with anything is beyond me." She checked her
tone abruptly. Julia looked wretched. The steel-blue eyes
were surrounded by flesh that was too gray and wrinkles
that were too pronounced. The car was cool, yet there
was moisture on Julia's forehead and her hands were
limp. Her lip color was a bluish purple. "Sweetheart,"
Trisha said quietly, "you want to see Kern, and we're
going to see him. We'll be there in an hour. Now I want
you to relax and stop worrying. There's no reason—"

"So you keep saying. But there is reason. I told you.
If he told me he had a concussion and broken ribs, God
knows what really happened! He is my son, Patricia,
even if we don't get along—"

"As in brick wall meeting brick wall," Trisha murmured under her breath.

Julia's jaw stiffened, her fingers plucking irritably at
the expensive silk material of her skirt. "You could try
to see it from my point of view. If he were your son,
Patricia, and you knew he was in trouble—"

"The day Kern has trouble he can't handle you can
count on the earth caving in, Julia. If anyone should be

doing any worrying in the Lowery family, it's him for you, not the other way around." There was really no point in arguing. One didn't argue with Julia. One either gave in promptly and with good grace, or one donned earmuffs and said no at persistent five-minute intervals, never giving an inch. There had been no stopping Julia once Kern evidently let slip on the telephone that he had been in an accident some weeks before. Knowing her son didn't want her there was fuel enough for Julia to go to him. And knowing that Trisha had no desire to see her husband after five long years—well, Julia had the gift of being immovably single-minded at times. And with her health as it was, Trisha knew she had no choice.

The road curled like a lariat and suddenly loped out straight, with a waterfall to the left and on the right the froth of a stream that rushed over gilt-edged rocks. The countryside was virgin primitive, lushly sensual at first glance, soft in color and scent and sound. It was all part of a dream she'd wanted to share with Kern once. Instead, Trisha thought fleetingly, there had been the harsh reality of living in it.

"He won't even recognize you," Julia murmured. "You'll be like two strangers meeting again. That's *really* why you're still irritated with me, Trisha, because you're afraid it will be awkward for you. But you can handle it . . ." Her voice trailed off at Trisha's startled expression. "Perhaps we'll just let that subject be."

"Perhaps we will!"

Trisha needed no reminder of how much she'd changed in the last five years. The cream silk pantsuit suit was sophisticated, designed to make the most of her slender figure and ivory skin. Her face was lovely in a fragile, ethereal way. Deep-set eyes were almond shaped, the color of sapphire, and her dark-gold hair was thick, swept back to curl on her shoulders. There was no sign at all of the girl she had been five years before, no bundle of nerves, no edge of tears, no telltale sign even to Julia that in any way she dreaded having to meet Kern after all this time. She looked the sophisticated twenty-five-year-old from Grosse Pointe that she was. No one would ever mistake her for a mountain girl.

"I've barely seen a house in an hour," Julia remarked suddenly.

"And we probably won't, darling, until we reach Kern's. But you'll find Grosse Pointe prices at Gatlinburg, I promise you, and that's only half an hour past Kern's. It's a lovely little town." It was a town set in the valley at the entrance to the Smoky Mountains. She remembered it well. Her palms were damp on the steering wheel, Trisha discovered, and she was disgusted with herself. She was miles, centuries away from the Trisha she had been at twenty, frightened of her own shadow, carting the word *love* around as if it had a halo that came with it. She had been a bit of fluff just asking to be crushed.

"How much longer?" Julia accused her wearily. "You said we'd be there."

Trisha shot her mother-in-law a sharp, worried glance. "And we will be. Just a few more minutes, that's all. Please relax, darling."

The road twisted past the campgrounds Kern had built. There were campers and trailers parked, although it was early yet, the end of May. Up past the shaded campgrounds the road twisted like a black ribbon with a meandering silver stream on the right. Above were the forest acres bedded with trillium and rhododendron, the scent overpowering on one stretch of the drive. And last was Kern's place...

No.

Like a knot of cold steel inside, Trisha felt a sudden panic tighten and chill. His kingdom. His corner that captured the real soul of the mountain country, where a century before a man might have died if he hadn't had the character to survive. She hadn't, she knew. But now she realized it wasn't really a fear of seeing Kern again that had filled her with dread. It was just the old sensation of feeling on trial—and failing . . .

Trisha shut off the engine and exhaled deeply. The house was completely different. It had been a skeleton when she left. Now the two rambling levels fit into the mountainside perfectly, as he had promised they would. The glass windows were scaled to perfection so that nothing marred Kern's view of the mountains beyond. Century-old mountain maples shaded three sides. Azaleas and ferns, which naturally decorated the woods beyond, bordered the stone walk to the front door. The natural peace and privacy of the place spoke of Kern in a thousand ways.

"Perhaps," Julia said quietly, "we could just start back right now. Right this minute."

"You're not serious." Trisha turned away from the memory-invoking landscape.

"Perhaps I was wrong, Patricia," her mother-in-law admitted with unaccustomed humility, a gray sheen of weariness painted on her complexion. "You never told me what it was like, and Kern's always been the one to visit me. I didn't know. There isn't a theater or a decent restaurant, no industry, no . . . darling, this is a wilderness! This is no place for you. If I'd known . . ."

For a moment Trisha was surprised that Julia felt no appreciation for the lush beautiful countryside, and then she reminded herself swiftly that they were both city

women. Her desire for cosmopolitan comforts was just
as strong as Julia's. "You should have seen it five years
ago," Trisha responded lightly. "I did warn you you
wouldn't want to stay, darling. There are no servants,
no garden clubs, no formal dinner hour. The idea of your
actually coming here to help Kern, when we both know
you haven't been face to face with a frying pan in thirty
years..."

"You won't just leave me here," Julia insisted weakly.

"I'll do just as I said. Come on Julia. I'll have you
comfortable in no time; then you'll forget all about the
long drive. When you're settled in, I'll go down to a
motel in Gatlinburgh. All you have to do is call whenever
you want to go home."

Trisha stretched as she got out of the car and took a
second look around. It must have rained that morning.
The forest smells were pervasive, the green hues sharp
and glistening. She moved to Julia's side of the car, trying
to deny the fresh pull on her senses that the country
invoked. "It will all look different once you've had a
rest..."

Julia was several inches taller than Trisha, and stiff
from the long drive. Trisha slipped an arm around her
waist to help her.

"I don't feel up to dealing with Kern," Julia admitted.
"I should have called him. You were right, Trisha. He's
going to be very angry, but I knew he wouldn't want me
to come..."

"There is nothing at all for you to worry about. I'll
deal with Kern," Trisha assured her, hearing the little
comment echo back with a tinge of irony. She hadn't
been able to handle Kern five years ago.

Inside the house a cool breeze fluttered at the draperies. Trisha remembered the bare boards and bare walls

in the huge living room. It was nothing like that now.
The thick luxurious carpet was pine green, and the long
low pair of couches and chairs were a complimentary
leaf-green shade. A knarled tree root had been varnished
and covered with a round glass top to form a coffee table.
Native limestone climbed the south wall in a massive
fireplace that dominated the room. Filled bookcases
reached the ceiling. The room was perfect, and that fact
irritated her in a completely irrational way.

"Kern?" Trisha called out. She moved with the weary
Julia past the living room to a small room beyond.

"I really don't feel well."

"I know you don't." The room was a good-sized rec-
tangle with a charming little alcove, bare but adequate
with a twin bed and an oak chest of drawers. "This will
do for now, Julia. The point is just to get you comfortable." She dealt first with Julia's purse, then loosened
the zipper of the silk dress and leaned over to take off
the older woman's shoes. As she was kneeling on the
hardwood floor, she felt Kern behind her.

"Mother? What on earth are you doing here? And
who . . ."

He never finished the sentence. Trisha turned her face
up to his and relished the few moments when he still
didn't recognize her. The last time she had seen Kern
she had been in torn jeans and one of his cast-off shirts,
looking twelve and feeling ninety, with hair unwashed
and exhaustion in purple swirls under her eyes. Suddenly
she remembered it very well.

She remembered how Kern had looked at the time
too. He had worn jeans and a red flannel shirt, and he
looked perfect in them because Kern had looked damned-
well perfect all the time.

He did not look perfect now.

Her eyes scanned the familiar territory. His face was strong and square, with ragged eyebrows and a jutting chin that was covered with more than the beginnings of a curling, bristly beard. The soot-black hair was thick and still inclined to resist the taming of a brush. His hawk eyes had the same piercing quality, the color and sheen of old pewter. The overall image was the same: power and pride. He claimed several inches above six feet and there was no stinting on the frame. His height, the beard, and the single hand on a hip all added up to the most primitive sort of man.

But it was the new territory that shocked Trisha to total stillness. A wretchedly jagged scar was far too close to his right eye, and still so red that the stitches could not have been long removed. The hollows beneath his eyes spoke of weariness and his right wrist was swathed in cream, the bandage held in place with a sling. Perhaps in some ridiculously irrational way Trisha had never really believed that he had been hurt. To her, Kern had always been like his mountain—immovable, unhurtable, unbeatable. She had never been able to picture him as vulnerable, as she had once been so very vulnerable.

"Lord, I'm sorry, Kern," she said, then turned from him and finished with Julia's shoes, disbelieving the odd tearlike sensation in her eyes. She had never wished him ill. "This is awkward for you. I'm sorry. I hadn't really planned on you're having to see me at all, but your mother wasn't well..." She cast a quick look at her mother-in-law and registered that Julia was for unknown reasons looking speculatively at her and not her son. "Julia was so worried about you that there was no stopping her, and rather than have her drive on her own, I just didn't see any choice..."

Talk, Julia, she felt like saying. *Carry the ball for*

me for just one minute! But Julia was content to have her dress slipped off by Trisha's efficient fingers and be settled beneath the sheet with a light blanket.

"She claims to have a perfect bill of health from the doctor she saw last Friday," Trisha said to the unmoving form behind her, as she carelessly swirled back a strand of gold that had slipped from her chignon. "I'll just get her some tea . . . if you don't mind?" She turned back to Kern, with a poised half smile on her lips that apologized for the intrusion but nothing more. She knew how to hide nerves these days, knew how to hide how unsettled she really felt being so close to him again.

Their eyes met for just one moment. If he was stunned at finally recognizing her, it didn't show. From the top of her gold crown to the gold-tipped sandals on her feet, his eyes swept over the very real changes in Trisha's looks. There was no smile. She couldn't read his expression, but there was an instant when a spark of emotion older than time flared in his eyes and she could feel her control slipping. The appraisal was frankly sexual. There had never been anyone but Kern who had the appalling skill of making her skin feel touched with a simple look. She drew in her breath and repeated, "If you don't mind, Kern? If you would prefer that I just leave . . ."

"What I'd like is a cup of coffee myself," he said finally.

"Fine. I have to admit you look—" She stopped uncomfortably.

"Like hell?" He finished for her.

The corner of her lips lifted, just a little. His slash of a smile held the same memory hers did. Hell had the inevitable devil in it, and when Trisha had first met Kern that was exactly how she had labeled him. And for good reason . . .

Kern stayed with his mother while Trisha found her way to the kitchen. She opened cupboards to find the accoutrements for tea, barely conscious of how much the room itself had changed. The colors were burnt orange and copper; every appliance and convenience shined with care. The long window over the sink held a view of the garden and the stretch of woods beyond, carpeted with spring violets. In front of her eyes was a picture that wouldn't go away. It was a picture of Kern and the night she had totally and whimsically fallen in the love with one tall, dark-eyed man, her devil of a man . . .

2

It was a New Year's Eve party at the Grosse Pointe Yacht Club on Lake Saint Clair. The ballroom was crowded, an overwhelming assault on the senses of festive lights and colorful couture gowns, cigarette smoke and champagne. A band in tuxedos played loudly over the high-pitched laughter, and increasingly boisterous conversation. The younger set of women were as scantily dressed as possible; the older, richly ornate in jewels and brocades.

Trisha wore a pale-blue floor-length gown that had cost the earth and did not suit the gathering at all. Medieval in design, the velvet came to a long low V at her wrists and ruffled demurely at the neck, draping loosely over her slim figure. She looked like an innocent princess, but that wasn't a picture that belonged in the sophisticated world of Grosse Pointe.

Her uncle had deserted her upon their arrival, which was not unexpected. It was typical of how he had raised her once her parents had died. Her uncle was not ungenerous; the material advantages were always there. But he was cold and indifferent far beyond the point of mere insensitivity. As a result Trisha was painfully shy and almost unforgivably naive for a girl of nineteen, a dreamer in mind and in looks.

The yacht club had dozens of rooms beyond the ballroom. There was a choice of three bands, a place to play poker, a room for conversation, and plenty of champagne everywhere. She wandered about slowly, feeling lost and uncomfortable. She hadn't wanted to come. At last she ventured to the third floor of the club, seeking refuge from the constant noise. Tentatively she opened a door to a dim, quiet room. The only light was from the moon which streamed in through the windows at the far end of the room, overlooking the ice-encrusted lake.

"Close it!"

She jumped in shock at the reverberating command that came from nowhere.

"I said close it!"

She closed it quickly, her heart beating wildly. Hours later she had wondered why she hadn't had the sense to close the door with herself on the opposite side. As it was, the party noise dulled to a distant hum and she leaned against the door, trying to fathom where the voice was coming from.

"Over here."

Cautiously she moved closer until her eyes adjusted to the darkness. When he struck a match to light a cigarette she was startled and her imagination worked overtime: it was surely the devil's face. He was stretched half out on the floor, leaning lazily against the wall, the cigarette in his one hand and a drink—and bottle—on the floor beside him.

There was no question that someone had made a terrible mistake trying to fit him out in powder blue. Black was clearly his color. He practically had more legs than there was carpet space and the breadth of his shoulders was just as daunting. The giant came equipped with a wicked pair of bushy eyebrows and dark eyes that radiated danger. She smiled politely and backed up as rapidly as her stiff legs would allow until she bumped into something, and he started laughing.

"I just bite necks, and that's only when there's a full moon. Although come to think of it . . ." He motioned to the window and the full white moon sitting low over the lake. "Never mind. Come and sit down if you're here to escape from that madhouse."

"Just for a minute," she said weakly, with a careful glance to insure she knew exactly where the door was. When she turned back he was smiling, and that soft sensual smile mesmerized her as he motioned her closer. Captivated, a bit frightened, she knelt on the carpet a little distance from him.

"You have blue eyes, don't you?" he asked idly as he poured her a glass of the amber-colored liquor.

She nodded, staring at the bottle.

"I'm not drunk," he told her perceptively. "They're serving champagne downstairs and I don't drink it. This is my second whiskey—from the look of you, your first."

She sipped at his whiskey, tiny sips so she wouldn't gag. Quiet reigned for a long time. She found herself unable to stop staring at him, aware but not self-conscious that he was studying her just as intently. She saw a brooding man, intense, and private. Arrestingly attractive though not really at all handsome. Disturbingly sexual and comfortable with power. "Why?" she asked quietly.

"Pardon?"

"Why are you getting drunk?"

He twirled the liquid in his glass, staring at her. "It's New Year's Eve."

She shook her head. "That's why they're drinking." She motioned downstairs. "That's not why you are. Of course it's none of my business. For that matter if you want me to go..." She made to get up again but his long arm reached out, a mammoth hand enclosing hers in a small, unexpectedly sensual little prison.

"Stay." The *please* was there, though he didn't say it. She felt loneliness—something she understood very well. She had the impulse to flee. This man spelled danger. She was out of her league. But the urge faded and she had the strange desire to comfort and soothe.

He took so long to answer that she was certain he wasn't going to. When he did, his voice was gruff and impatient. "I've just had enough of cement and pollution...of using people like rungs on a ladder." He was looking out over the lake, not at her. "But in a year or two I very well may not care anymore. There was an article in yesterday's paper. My company, taking over another. A 'financial coup' they labeled it." He shook his head. "What it was was taking advantage of another man when he's down."

He talked—a world completely foreign to her, but it didn't matter. She was listening to him on another level entirely. So cynical, so hard, the words spit out from him as if he'd forgotten how to talk about his feelings. "Don't do it then," she said simply. "Do something else. Something that you want—that you *need*."

"God, you sound young," he said dryly. He reached beside him to switch on a small table lamp. She felt his eyes sweep over her as if they were fingers, assessing the quality of her dress, her hair, her skin. She shivered uncomfortably, wary of the sensual appraisal again and yet strangely compelled to sit still for it. He had admitted he was a predator, but she did not feel like prey. His face seemed to soften the more he stared. "It isn't just young in years, is it?" he asked probing quietly. "It's in those bright eyes. We still believe in rainbows, do we? Happy endings? Love?"

She lifted her chin. "I get up every day glad to be alive. How about you?"

He hesitated, then chuckled dryly. "Perhaps there's a case for naiveté."

His insolence sparked a rare spurt of temper. "Mister—whatever your name is—I saw both my parents killed five years ago in a car crash. Don't you go telling me I don't know what life's about. I'd still rather look up than down any day. It's a question of choice. If you haven't made it, I feel sorry for you!"

The door snapped open at the far end of the room; two drunken revelers trying to find privacy. "Get out of here," the stranger snapped, making Trisha jump warily at the instant autocratic order in his voice. They left promptly, and Trisha, suddenly uneasy, stirred to get up.

"Stay."

"I don't think so."

"Stay. I have a mountain I want to tell you about. If you're so young that you still believe in dreams you should like hearing about it."

She fell in love hearing about it. At midnight there were New Year's fireworks, shouts, and a hullabaloo from below that destroyed their conversation. The tall dark man stopped talking, pulled her up from her sitting position, and held her hand as they watched the fireworks over Lake Saint Clair from the window. When he turned to her finally, every instinct already guessed what he was going to do. The dark grave look in his eyes was oddly possessive, searing as his face moved closer. The secrets shared, of dreams both wanted to believe in, felt like the kiss that happened. She had never felt as protected as she did with his arms around her, the first sweet yearnings of desire burning inside of her.

Sometime after that the raucous dance music slowed and mellowed for the tired, thinning crowd below. Old nostalgic love songs floated into the hushed dark room. For two hours they danced alone in the stillness. On occasion he would lift her head and just look at her, and she held nothing back in the way she looked back at him. She wasn't so young that she didn't realize she could be hurt; she just didn't care. He was a man of dreams, a man to protect as she had never felt protected. She felt cherished, desired. She curled close like a kitten, her arms around his waist, her forehead against the soft new bristle of beard forming on his chin at the late hour.

Three weeks later he met with her uncle, while Trisha waited outside the study wringing her hands. The wedding was hastily planned. But there was no choice. He had come to the breaking point in his executive world. A merger had been accomplished that would move him from the president's chair to the chairman's seat, permitting him to maintain his finger in all the Lowery pies but enabling him to relinquish direct control. It was his chance. She understood. He was free, and he wasn't willing to wait any longer for anything he really wanted. If she really believed in his dream of the mountains, she had to go with him now. There would be no second chances with a man like Kern.

It was after midnight when Kern emerged alone and angry from her uncle's study. He caught her up in that dark hall and pressed his mouth on hers until her neck ached and she felt dizzy and frightened and deliciously possessed. When he let her go she held onto his arms, too shy even to look at him. "I can't get you out of this house soon enough, Tish," he said gratingly. "Your uncle's got a lot to answer for as far as you're concerned, the cold-blooded..." He shook his head, and his voice lowered, using the gentler tone he always used with her. "I need you, Tish. You're pure nectar to me, almost too pure...I know it's too soon for you, but you're better off with me than where you are now. We'll make it work. I know you're young, Tish, but I can't wait. Won't..."

Kern had been impatient through the ceremony, impatient with his mother, impatient still to be in the city they were leaving on the morrow. He had piled two weeks of work into a single week. She understood his urgency, but he was different...a stranger. Kern was used to making mountains move at the snap of his fingers, but Tish knew only the quieter, the gentler man.

The honeymoon suite was lavish, with thick gold carpeting and filled with flowers. They had a view of the Detroit River at night. He had ordered a late dinner to be sent up to the room and then turned around and canceled it. He had sat on the bed and watched her standing still at the window, looking out. In the pale pink silky dress, her profile delicate, her shining gold hair hanging almost to her waist, her unsureness was a fragile and lovely portrait to him. "Come here, Tish." She had looked at him with frozen eyes, and he had smiled, motioning her closer. "It will be all right." He had come to her, bent her cheek to his chest and slowly unzipped the dress, kissing her forehead when he felt her trembling. "I love you, Tish...it's going to be all right..."

But it wasn't. Kern was still impatient and she knew

it. She lost all of her confidence with her clothes, and Kern, formidable in his tailored suits, stripped off his civilized veneer when he took them off. Suddenly there was so much of him all at once, so much intimacy all at once. Wanting desperately to please him and not having the least idea how, she felt more sick than sensual, and Kern had been on fire. A primitive wildfire she had never guessed at was inside him, earthy in lust, with none of the control she had seen in him before.

The pain was a shock and she had struggled mindlessly to get away from the stranger that was Kern. He had hushed her, soothed her, tried to be gentle, but she sensed he was unhappy with her responses. And she couldn't blame him. When it was over, she knew it hadn't been right and was almost out of her mind with unhappiness, for his sake, for theirs. Until then she had a tentative but very optimistic confidence that she was a mate for Kern, that he needed her softness and gentle understanding to bring him strength, to be the kind of man he wanted to be. After that it was downhill.

The mountain was fantastically beautiful, better than her dream, but living there had been a nightmare. There was only a cold-water well that had to be pumped and a cabin to camp out in while Kern set about building the house. He didn't want to live off the Lowerys so he set up a campground for the trailer trade, in order for them to be self-sufficient. It was all he wanted, the hard work didn't daunt him. He was happy. Happy with everything but his new wife.

She was becoming obsessively sure of that. He worked sixteen-hour days in which she barely saw him. Rationally she understood it would have to be that way at the start. Emotionally she couldn't cope. She didn't know how to keep house in the primitive conditions. She didn't know how to cook, much less on a wood stove. She was painfully shy with the strangers and local people. And she hadn't been prepared for the snakes and bears. By the end of the day she was as exhausted as he, and when they came together at night she was frozen with the fear that she wouldn't please him. Passion and anxiety were not a blend that went well together, and every morning she looked up at the tall, virile, healthy man that was her husband and saw his eyes shying away from her.

It was then that she had walked out. Emotionally destroyed, a bundle of inadequacy, a pale wraith of the fragile loveliness she once was. All the pieces had to be put back together because she was shattered, and it had taken a long time. She had not pursued a divorce. She didn't want that piece of paper that would have given her her freedom. The thin band of gold had stayed on her finger. Not because she had any illusions of getting back with Kern, but because it served as a protection and kept other men away.

With Julia's help in the beginning she had made it on her own. She was proud of her job and the life she had made for herself. The confidence she had in herself was real this time, not based on dreams.

The kettle whistled, and Trisha removed it from the burner. Just for a moment, seeing Kern hurt had brought back the old memories of a strong man who had his moments of vulnerability, who she had believed even needed her. Of course he really didn't then and he certainly didn't now.

"Damn it. I've been trying to get my mother here for ages. But not *now*, Tish."

Trisha was reaching into the refrigerator. She straightened at the sound of his voice, bringing out a package of cheese. "So you talked to her." She kept her face averted, slicing the cheese wafer-thin, making tiny sandwiches for Julia that she knew would please.

"I told her there was nothing wrong with me. I don't understand why she had to hightail it out here from Grosse Pointe, and I don't understand why she looks so awful. I just spoke to her on the phone last Sunday. She was 'marvelous, darling,'" Kern quoted.

Trisha piled the little quarter sandwiches on a tray and bent to seek some sort of relish from the fridge plus parsley and olives, which Julia loved. "She fibs, Kern. Pit her against the average four-year old and you could probably have a contest," Trisha said calmly.

His smile was swift, like fresh air. She caught just a glimpse of it as she turned back to the tray. The deep-set gray eyes had almost pinned hers, and Trisha thought how like the mountain cats he was. The easy, sure movements. The eyes always alert. The subtlety of muscle cloaked in that golden skin of his. The scars and bandages took nothing away from him but added an unexpected illusion of human frailty. She felt disturbed as he watched her making the tea. "I don't know what to tell you," she added finally.

"Well, I can't handle her now. People are flooding into the camp this season and I'm behind because of the ridiculous accident. Sit down for a minute, will you?" He scraped back a kitchen chair and waited.

She didn't want to sit. She wanted to take the tray back to Julia and leave, quickly, but she couldn't justify that kind of cowardice in her own mind. After pouring two cups of coffee, her own half full, she took the chair across from him.

"You're going to have to stay until she's ready to go home."

It was what she had planned all along, but it sounded different coming from Kern, as if what he was talking about was staying with *him*. "Well, of course. After I have Julia settled, I'm going down to Gatlinburg to get a motel—"

"There's three bedrooms upstairs. Don't be ridiculous." He lifted the cup and took a long sip of the bitter hot coffee, staring at her over the rim. "I barely recognized you when you walked in," he said quietly. "I understand you've got quite an impressive job these days."

"An assistant buyer at Markham's is hardly impressive, Kern. But I like it," she murmured, stirring a spoon into the coffee she didn't really want.

"You went to school at night for two years. Started as a salesclerk. I'd call it impressive to start from nowhere and end up at the place you are. Mother told me you've got your own place, close to the river," he continued. "When I first met you I never thought you'd be happy living in the city, but you're right in the heart of it, aren't you? And those rents aren't inexpensive."

"Yes," she said flatly. So he had made a point of knowing what she'd been up to. Why? Rapidly she switched the subject. "How badly were you hurt? It was a car accident, wasn't it?"

He grimaced. "The mountain roads weren't meant for drag racers. It was a couple of kids. One of them got a broken leg and the other lost a few teeth. It could have been worse."

"And what about you?"

"A few cuts and scrapes. Nothing."

The scar on his forehead and bandaged wrist weren't "nothing." Julia had spoken of a concussion and broken ribs. Still, it was typical of Kern to downplay his own hurts, and as far as wanting to share with her—well, of course he wouldn't. "The camp looks double the size it was before. And the house..."

"Naturally, it's finished," Kern said curtly. "You stayed with mother for a time after you left?"

Unconsciously she reached to smooth back a tendril of hair that brushed her cheek. "Yes," she admitted a little ruefully. "I certainly didn't intend to. When Uncle Nate moved from Grosse Pointe to California, he left a few boxes of my things with Julia, because she was closer—"

"And it was a lot less trouble than having to mail them here," Kern interrupted dryly. "God forbid he should ever have had to go out of his way for you."

Trisha gave a little shrug, surprised he had remembered her uncle at all. "It wasn't his fault he had an orphan thrust on him when my parents died. I hadn't planned to go back to live with him nor your mother. It was just a question of going to her house to pick up my things. But the day I went it was raining and I had a halfhearted case of flu. The next thing I knew—"

"Mother had taken you over."

"With appalling speed." Trisha shook her head. "Well, I *was* ill, and then later it was a question of getting on my feet with a job. Talking to Julia about my leaving was like arguing with a brick wall. But whether or not you believe me, Kern, I grew to care for her very much and still do. Once I got past that formidable exterior..." She stopped, rather appalled that she was telling him so much so easily.

Kern leaned forward. "Go on," he said, encouraging her.

"Well...I invited her to dinner after I was set up in the apartment. She was so shocked—as if she thought

I'd just forget her once I left. Apart from my being an indifferent cook at best in those days, I don't think anyone had had the nerve to serve Julia spaghetti in years. Much less invite her to a place decorated in early attic," Trisha said dryly. "I remembered that she was fussy about salad dressings so I made a Jell-o molded salad. No one can mess up one of those. Only . . ."

The corner of his mouth was twitching. She felt an odd stirring inside to see that slash of a smile. "Go on."

"I had molded it beautifully," Trisha said frankly. "Only I seemed to have molded in the spoon I'd stirred it with. She never said a word. When she offered to serve the salad I just said yes, and it was only after she was gone and I was cleaning up that I saw she had carved very carefully around the spoon . . ."

He had such a delicious chuckle, throaty and vibrant. Trisha smiled back, an unexpected warmth curling all through her at the sound of him. His eyes softened in laughter, the corners crinkling in little fan lines, and when he stopped smiling the sensual softness was still there when he looked at her.

"Anyway, she took care of me for a time, and I found myself reversing the role, taking care of Julia from time to time. I didn't think you'd mind, Kern. Julia never even brought up the two of us. And when she was determined to come down here and see you, I couldn't say no to her."

Kern stood up to take his empty coffee cup to the sink. She'd deliberately tried to provoke his laughter with the silly little story, and she had. Five years ago there was none, and suddenly his laughter was a reminder of how they might have related to each other. She stood up, too, and took a breath.

"Well, I'd better get this tray to your mother," she said briskly. "I may just stay here tonight, Kern, if you really don't mind. Then by morning if Julia's better I can have us both out of your hair quickly—"

The vice of his fingers suddenly grasped her wrist. Her shocked face stared up in amazement at his instant change in mood. Hawk eyes seared hers. "So we managed fifteen minutes of casual conversation. We almost sound like old friends, Tish," he said sarcastically. "Very cool, very relaxed, very poised, Trisha. Not at all the way you used to be!"

His work-roughened hand did odd things to the soft skin of her own. "It's still there, I see. I saw it the minute you came in."

The slim gold band seemed to wink at both of them. For a moment she looked up at Kern, her eyes like two blue ink drops on snow. Her face had whitened, not because of the sudden rough contact, but because her senses were unexpectedly assaulted by the closeness of him. He was such a sexual man. The piratelike beard enclosing a mouth that was incredibly smooth-textured. The outdoor scent that was uniquely a part of him. The careless array of thick black hair around a face whose expression was never careless, always alert, always perceptive...

He released his hold. "I waited for you to apply for a divorce."

"I thought you would, Kern. In the beginning I didn't have the money for it, and...it never really mattered, not when we both knew it was over. I—" Her voice was barely audible. The longer she stared at him, the more she felt mesmerized by the gray light of his eyes, strangely soft for an instant and sad. Bitterly sad for what they both wanted from each other once, and Trisha ached to be closer suddenly, to reach out and just hold him, and be held.

There was a sharp rap on the door behind her, and Kern stepped around her to answer it.

"Sorry I'm late, honey. I—oh!"

The woman had her arms extended with the obvious intention of giving Kern a hug of greeting, until she caught sight of Trisha standing there. It did not take thirty seconds for the scene to gel in Trisha's mind. If Kern had broken every limb there would still have been no need for Julia to come help. He was obviously being well taken care of.

The lady was a well-curved Amazon with the black eyes and black hair of their Cherokee neighbors. Tight jeans were molded over long legs. A red T-shirt, worn braless, hid nothing of her voluptuous figure, and an incredibly long swath of loose hair flowed to her waist. Her skin was the bronze of an outdoor woman...a mountain woman. A very sexy woman in a natural way, with probably a few years over Trisha. At that particular moment very little seemed to matter.

Trisha swallowed the ridiculous lump in her throat and stepped forward with a slim hand extended in greeting. "I'm Trisha Lowery," she said pleasantly. "An unexpected visitor of Kern's."

"Rhea Andreas." The woman acknowledged the handshake with another careful look at Kern. "I was coming to fix Kern's dinner, but—"

"I was wondering how he managed without his right hand," Trisha said cheerfully as she picked up Julia's tray. "It was nice meeting you, Rhea. I'm on my way—out of the way."

"Tish—"

"Have a good dinner," she urged, and with a bright smile aimed somewhere between the two of them, briskly headed out the door and back to Julia's room.

"I think we'd better plan on leaving first thing in the morning," Trisha said promptly, as she angled the tray onto Julia's lap.

3

JULIA CLOSED HER EYES. "My blood pressure's up. I can feel it. Could you get my pills from the suitcase, Trisha?"

By the time Trisha returned with the suitcase, Julia had eaten the sandwiches and finished the tea. "How I hate it when I don't feel well," she said testily. "Such a nuisance. Especially now."

"Kern will know a doctor—"

"Over my dead body."

Trisha let it be. Julia, however formidable with her Grosse Pointe symphony set, was never going to be a match for her son. And Kern would brook no such nonsense if he thought Julia needed a doctor in the morning. "Perhaps you'll feel better after you've had a good night's sleep. But if you don't feel up to going home in the morning, darling, I think I will go back alone. It's not that monstrous a drive to come and get you later—"

"I never heard of anything so ridiculous," Julia snapped. "You've got a month's leave, Trisha. Kern isn't as badly off as I was afraid of, but I still want to stay a day or two now that we've come all this way. You can't just go home!"

"I can't stay here." The words just slipped out. She had no right to feel shock at the sight of the woman Rhea. But telling herself she was a fool suddenly to feel like splintered glass didn't help. Before she arrived she had never, never had any expectations where Kern was concerned.

"Trisha, you must be curious after all this time," Julia said. "Don't tell me the situation is the same as it was before. *You're* not the same. I've waited and waited..."

Trisha's jaw dropped. There had been no hint in five years that Julia had ever wished the two of them back together. Julia was the one who had coddled her Grosse Pointe style, decrying everything about the mountain life her son had chosen. "Exactly *what* have you been waiting for?" Trisha demanded.

Julia's eyes shuttered, and she fussed with the blanket pulled to her chest. "You could do it now, Patricia. Convince him to come back home. You could have persuaded him before, but now... You're a much more beautiful woman. You've got grace and style and confidence. I don't blame you for hating all this—this primitive country—but if you were both back home..."

"Lord, I don't believe this!"

Julia regarded her with utter calm. For a moment Trisha even wondered if Julia had arranged for the bluish tinge on her lips, the odd little half breaths, the physical weakness. And then she felt horribly guilty for the thought. "Oh, Julia," she scolded wearily. "That really isn't why you insisted on making this trip, is it?"

"I wanted to know how Kern was, of course. But Roberts could have driven me. There must be some reason I have a chauffeur," Julia said reasonably.

"You told me his family was ill."

"Hmmmm."

Trisha rolled her eyes to the ceiling in exasperation. "Neither of us has been carrying a torch all this time. How could you even think it!"

"You've never gotten a divorce."

"That's just a piece of paper!"

"So's a marriage certificate. But you kept that," Julia said pleasantly.

"That's completely different. I knew I never wanted to marry again; there just wasn't any point..."

"All right," Julia said calmly, her eyes so shrewdly assessing that Trisha had the urge to shake her. "Whatever you say, darling. But all I want to do is spend a couple of days. You can't desert me when we've come this far. At least wait until I feel a little better."

"Wrong, Julia. That's just what you have a son for. I'm leaving in the morning."

Trisha refused to listen any further. Julia was tucked in, the curtains pulled closed, her case unpacked for her, and the tray taken care of. By the time Trisha finally left the room, Julia's eyes were closing.

Wearily Trisha wandered outside, her hands dug in the pockets of her cream silk slacks. For a few minutes she simply refused to think about Kern or Julia, or Rhea. She was exhausted, disturbed and unsettled inside.

The peace of the evening reached out to her like a gift. The peaks were silhouetted in the brilliant flame colors of the falling sun. The pine trees studding the mountains took on burnished hues...she had expected no peace, but it was there suddenly, and her rapid stride slowed.

Her feet automatically took a certain trail. There was a waterfall she remembered, a secret place, too far to reach this night, but the direction was instinctive. She took her hands from her pockets and hugged her arms against the evening chill. The trees cradled her in shade, rustling whispers just above her. Just once she wanted to remember this country without anguish, without memories, just to savor the old dreams . . .

The night sounds began suddenly—the eager restless rustlings of animals who preferred the darkness to do their living. The Smokies were a protected area, for fauna and for animals. Possum, raccoon, white-tailed deer, wild turkey, and fox frequently ventured onto Kern's land. The animals and particularly the snakes that she had once been afraid of didn't affect her this night.

She walked an hour or more. It was a tar-black sky when she ventured back to Kern's, guided by patches of moonlight between the trees. Her sandals were soaked with dew by the time she returned. The breeze had tugged loose her chignon and gold strands of hair ribboned across her cheeks. She was chilled, bone weary, but more at peace from her solitary hour in the mountain night than she could ever remember. There was just something about the air. Light-headed, strangely euphoric, she plucked a white blossom as she crossed the clearing behind Kern's house, lifting it to smell the heavy sweet fragrance.

He was there, in the shadow of the doorway, perhaps a hundred yards away. All in black, the sling gone. She couldn't see his face or any of him clearly. But she knew it was Kern. She dropped the blossom, instinctively digging her hands in her pockets again. It was an effort to switch off that deliciously sensual mood and convert it to a cool, polite smile. "Kern?"

He started walking toward her, his eyes meeting hers in the darkness. A knot tightened in her chest. He looked so damned primitive, black on black, his eyes glinting silver. As he came closer, she was desperately trying to come up with some polite, safe conversation.

But he didn't talk. He just kept coming. Like the night closing in and an illusion of slow-motion time, he walked right up to her. The fingers of his left hand threaded through her hair and gently tugged. Her face was raised to moonlight, her lips already parted in shock.

He blocked out the stars, moon, and sky when his head bent to hers. His arms cloaked her chilled skin in vibrant warmth. His lips were soft, tantalizingly sensual next to the bristling texture of the beard. Her neck arched back, cradled in his left hand, her breast pressed against his chest.

It was so completely unexpected. She was still trying to think of polite things to say, still trying to pretend that the mountain night hadn't touched her with the promise of old dreams. His lips brushed hers, over and over, and then sank in thirstily. Her mouth was the vessel, open to the erotic exploration of his tongue, the sensual touch firing a strange ache and longing inside. For just a moment she was someone else, not the painfully inhibited Trisha who had fled from Kern's bed. She was just a woman, lost in the chilled night air, reaching out from loneliness to the one person who knew all about loneliness.

"Tish..."

The soft lips left hers, trailed to the sensitive skin of her neck. His fingers roamed slowly from the nape of her neck to her shoulder, gradually seeking the silky skin of her throat beneath the blouse's fabric. She heard a murmur escape from her lips and felt a frightening weakness as if she needed to hold on. Her hands found his waist, pressed into his flesh, and suddenly her heart was beating rapidly. He smelled so warm. None of it made sense. Confused, she tried to draw back.

"No, no. Not yet, Tish," he murmured. His mouth

covered hers just as his palm covered her heartbeat, then edged just inches over to claim the uptilted orb of her breast. Voltage shocked through her at his touch. Her breasts were small; suddenly they felt huge, almost painfully swelling in response. Her fingers dug into his skin and suddenly his head lifted from hers. Silvery dark eyes studied her.

She shivered, heard a low moan in the distant trees that reminded her of old fears...of failing him. Of a hundred embraces that had ended in disaster, even if they had not been quite like this one. But to put herself in that place again...She jerked back, clutching the collar of her blouse together.

Her voice quavered. "I don't believe you did that."

"And I don't believe how much you've changed."

She bit her lip as he followed her back into the house. Only in the dimly lit kitchen did she glance back at him. He just stood in the doorway, his one hand loosely massaging the back of his neck as if he were tired. But the look in his eyes wasn't at all tired. The look in his eyes frightened her. He knew she had responded; he knew it wasn't the same.

She pushed her hair back from her face and turned from him. If she were home, she would have had a cup of tea. After what just happened, she wondered shakily if he stocked any of the mountain-made whiskey.

She had had no dinner, but lunch had been eaten late on the road, and she knew she couldn't handle food right now anyway. She just needed something to put her to sleep, to settle her nerves. Grateful for his Lowery upbringing, Trisha found not whiskey in the cupboard but the finest Cognac. "Do you want a glass?"

He nodded silently. She poured for both of them, handed him his glass, and then backed deliberately to the counter by the door. There was less than an inch of fluid in her glass. She gulped half of it, staring out the dark window, and then moved resolutely toward the door.

"We're going to talk about it, Tish." His voice was low, as gentle as it was unmistakably a warning.

"No. Please no."

She took two more steps toward the door but his rapid pace beat hers. It was Kern who pushed the swinging door so she could pass through. A halo of light from the living room lit the hall. "I'll get your suitcase."

"I can get it." The green bag was still by the front door, carted in when Trisha had brought Julia's things.

Kern ignored her, snatching it up with his left hand, motioning her up the stairs. His features were taut, and she moved ahead of him, an absolute mess of confusion inside. What exactly *had* he wanted to talk about? Kisses? Divorces? She swallowed, and asked, "Are you supposed to be lifting anything?"

"There doesn't seem to be much in this anyway."

"One uncrushable dress and a nightgown. I didn't need much for a day-and-a-half drive," she said lightly.

The spare bedrooms were directly at the top of the stairs. At the far southern end of the house was the huge master bedroom that would have been theirs. She paused between the first two doors. "I don't know where you'd like me to stay."

"There's a choice of three." She didn't at all appreciate the humorous tone in his voice. Still, he stepped ahead of her to switch on the light on the eastern bedroom and set her suitcase down on a chair. "Rhea will have put clean sheets in here. She stayed when I had the concussion."

"Yes." Trisha moved to the window, thinking of the other woman taking care of Kern when he was ill. Kern bent to switch on the lamp by the four-poster bed and then moved to the door to switch off the glaring overhead light.

"I'll check on Mother." In the shadows she could still see the outline of the scar on his forehead, the way he held his right arm up parallel to his waist as if it were still in the sling. "I'll be downstairs for a while if you need anything else."

"Thank you. I didn't expect..."

His eyes honed onto her slim figure, the golden hair disheveled as much from his own fingers as from the wind. "What didn't you expect?"

She took a breath. The word came out awkwardly, before she had the chance to think. "Kindness."

"But then you never did, Tish," he said evenly. "As I said, we'll talk about it. But not now."

She let out a breath when the door closed behind him. In a few minutes she moved, flicking on the light in the adjoining bath. She had a nighttime ritual, as most people did. Her outfit was folded meticulously and placed in the suitcase, the dress taken out for the morrow and hung up. Her face was washed, a violet wisp of a nightgown put on, her hair brushed smooth. Her personality these days demanded order. There would be no rest until everything was put in its place. An idiotic habit, perhaps, but then for a long time loneliness had created insomnia. As she switched off the lamp and curled under strange sheets in the strange room, the neatness habit mocked her. Kern had been messy as all hell at night, his clothes stripped and left wherever they landed when he had been in a hurry to join her in their bedroom.

She sighed, closing her exhausted eyes deliberately, curling her leg just so and her shoulder in a certain pattern to assure sleep. A lump was lodged in her throat, an anguished knot of too many memories in that other bed-room. One short embrace in the night didn't change that. Only a fool would read something into a few simple kisses. She'd been exhausted, disoriented, not herself, she told herself wearily. Yet the question plagued her long into the night. Did he actually still want her?

At five minutes to six the next morning, Trisha tiptoed down the stairs, determined to have a cup of coffee in silence before either Kern or Julia woke up. Swinging from her hand was a pair of red sandals with ribbon-thin straps. The navy jersey she wore had red piping for trim and a slash of red belt that cinched in her narrow waist. The dress was an old favorite and she loved the way the material flowed softly around her knees when she walked; more relevant at the moment was that it was unbeatable to travel in. Going home was the second on the list of priorities, directly after coffee.

She slipped on the sandals at the closed door to the kitchen and stifled a yawn. An early riser by nature when she was rested, she found it difficult to wake after a long, restless night. She pushed open the swinging door and two startled pair of eyes met each other.

Rhea had a huge coffee pot in her hand. She, too, wore red and navy, a red chamois shirt and a tight pair of navy jeans. Besides the colors there was no resem-blance to be found between the two women. Rhea was the image of a country woman next to Trisha's crisp city freshness. "I—good morning," Rhea said hesitantly. "I was just making coffee."

"Good morning." The look of surprise was unmistak-able in Rhea's eyes. Kern evidently had neglected to mention he was having overnight guests. "I've been com-ing over to make Kern breakfast in the mornings. He hasn't been able to do much for himself with his right wrist out of commission. If you want something..."

It was just six o'clock but the floor already looked scrubbed and the dishes in the dishwasher from the night before had been put away. Trisha felt relieved that she had decided to go home this day. The lady was a prize, a living composite of all the things Trisha had not been once upon a time—efficient, devoted, marvelously beddable.

"I asked if I could get you anything?" Rhea repeated.

"I—yes." The bedroom-eyed brunette might even be nice, but every nerve in Trisha's body tensed defensively. She had no right to Kern, not after five years, but a cup of coffee in solitude surely wasn't too much to ask. She smiled stiffly at Rhea. "I'm leaving in a few hours with Kern's mother. If you don't mind, I can put on the pot of coffee myself. Mrs. Lowery is rather fussy and she hasn't been well, so I'd have to make her breakfast anyway—"

"Oh, but this isn't for—"

"I wouldn't mind," Trisha said with pleasant firmness.

"Well." Rhea was a good six inches taller than Trisha, but she backed down like a lamb. With a little shrug of her shoulders she set down the coffee pot. "You can tell Kern I'll see him later today."

"I'll be sure to do that."

With a pleasant smile Trisha closed the door on the none-too-happy Rhea. At the moment she wasn't too happy either and her smile faded as she turned back to the kitchen. The huge pot of coffee seemed an enormous amount for three people, but it was already started. Perhaps Kern had fallen into the habit of drinking coffee during the day.

Waiting for the coffee to finish perking, Trisha leaned on the counter, looking out the long low window over the sink. The sun was catching the dew from the grass and trees, glittering brightly on the exact spot where Kern had kissed her. The night had been full of that echoing image. She had barely slept. But in the morning light she had a sudden picture in her mind of Rhea and Kern in that same spot. Rhea, with her earthy looks and sleepy dark eyes, was a much more suitable mate for Kern than she had ever been.

She turned away when the pot finally finished perking and the steamy aroma pervaded the kitchen. She found a mug in the cupboard and was pouring herself a cup when the back door opened.

"Well, howdy, ma'am!"

The invader was a tall lanky westerner with mustache and wide-brimmed hat which he hastily removed. He was followed by a blonde little wren of a woman, then two men with fishing gear propped at the door, a freckled and pigtailed sprite of a child, a teenager with lazy green eyes, an austerely handsome grandfatherly and banker type, and finally Kern.

The morning light gave his eyes a smoky cast as they surveyed her from head to toe and back again, taking in everything from the chignon and startled expression to the tailored dress. His eyes fixed for a moment on her shapely legs and longer yet on the curve of her hips. He moved so quickly toward her that she froze, his look so damned sexual that it made her feel stalked.

"Just sit down everyone," he drawled lazily. "Have breakfast up in a minute. Nate, Barb, Robert, Ed, Mrs. Anther, little Georgia, Bill—this is Trisha. My wife." One other man entered the kitchen; a stocky blond about her own age with a pair of puppy-soft brown eyes. "And this is Jack, who has been living and working at the camp for the last three months. He's aiming toward a forestry degree."

She was trying to attach names to faces when Kern's hand brushed her shoulder. "Is the coffee ready? Where's Rhea?"

She thought it odd that he had introduced her as his wife, when it was bound to raise questions for him when she was gone. At the moment she simply set down her coffee, understanding all too quickly that Rhea had been trying to tell her she was there for more reasons than just Kern's coffee. "It didn't take two of us to handle a little breakfast," she murmured awkwardly.

"You mean she's gone? Why on earth would she take off now when she knew there would be a group coming in?"

Why on earth indeed? She flashed him an irritated look. Five years ago he had occasionally brought in people at a moment's notice. She had a clear-cut memory of six people waiting while she burned a dozen eggs and fled in tears from her failure. "How many heads?" Trisha called out over the sound of scraping chairs as people sat down.

"Eleven," volunteered the freckled urchin.

Kern was already lining up styrofoam cups on a counter. When he went to lift the heavy coffee pot with his left hand, it wobbled. "Just sit down," she ordered him under her breath.

"Look, Tish, no one asked you to do anything like this. You don't need to—"

"Hush, Kern," she whispered crisply, "and just get out of my way."

There was some sort of wretched humor in history

repeating itself, although this time around she at least knew what she was doing in a kitchen. The sausages were prepared for the microwave and coffee poured for eleven. Little Georgia was enlisted to carefully deliver the cups and the cream and sugar. Two dozen eggs were cracked, blended with milk, grated cheese, green pepper, and fresh pepper. The toast popped out in fours, was buttered and stashed in a warming oven as the eggs started cooking.

"Mrs. Lowery, if you should be wanting some help..." offered the fragile little blonde woman.

"Please call me Trisha. And there's nothing, really." As she set a knife and fork in front of Kern, he was talking about the hiking trails to one couple, wildflowers to another. He was answering every question about fishing, wildlife and mountain lore, but he was aware of her. She could feel it. There was the faintest hint of a smile in that beard that had nothing to do with the subjects at hand. Was he amused that she was coping so easily? Worse than that, she feared she was creating an impression of enjoying herself.

With a little pang she realized that she *was* enjoying herself, the chaos and good cooking smells, the diversity of people and laughter. It was only Kern who threw her, so irritably virile-looking in a gold pullover and tan pants, his skin like dark honey, his brilliantly alert eyes beneath bushy brows following her every movement.

She flew back to stir the eggs, took out the next round of toast, popped the microwave button for the sausages, and pulled out plates from the shelf. Five minutes later it was all served, and with one long sigh of satisfaction Trisha turned to pour herself that suddenly, desperately needed cup of coffee.

Kern's chair suddenly grated on the floor behind her.

"Sit here, Tish," he ordered. "You seem to have forgotten a plate for yourself. I'm already done."

She shook her head. "I never eat breakfast. All I want—"

His eyes glittered mischief. "Now, now. Just sit down." He laced his arm around her neck and propelled her forward to the table. "We've got to get you fed and out in the sun. You're city pale, sweets." His man Jack was staring curiously. He was the only one present who obviously should have known before about Kern's "wife." Trisha flushed, stiffly refusing to sit down for a meal she didn't want, awkward in front of so many eyes. Kern's palm smoothed down her spine, patted her fanny in what must have looked like affection and what felt distinctly like a shocking intimacy. She sat down promptly. "That's a good girl."

Are you ill? she said distinctly with her eyes, both angry and bewildered by his actions. It was obviously not the occasion to speak out loud, and in spite of herself in a few minutes she nearly forgot her irritation. Idaho, Wisconsin, Florida, New York, and Mississippi were represented at the table, plus CPAs, farmers, and a college professor. It was really an intriguing mix of people and she was drawn into their conversations, managing a bite or two of breakfast in between, again ruefully finding that she was enjoying herself.

Finally the group started filtering out. As Kern stood at the door answering last-minute questions, Trisha quickly jumped up to start shuffling dishes back into the dishwasher. In minutes she had been thrown pell mell into Kern's life again as if she belonged, and Kern's lazy familiarity confused her. Just what kind of game did he think he was playing?

With lightning speed she hurried to put the kitchen back in reasonable order, finally pausing to pour her second cup of cold coffee down the drain.

"I heard voices," Julia said reproachfully from the doorway.

"Morning, Mother," Kern's tone was casual, but his eyes were instantly and shrewdly assessing his mother's health just as Trisha's were.

Julia was dressed meticulously in one of her favored raw silks. Her hair was groomed strictly back and her eyes were steely blue . . . and battle-sharp ready. But the step was uneven and a makeup foundation could not hide the pallor of her complexion.

Unconsciously Trisha glanced at Kern, her eyes a soft mirror of worry and shared compassion she couldn't help. Truthfully she felt a measure of relief that Kern would handle his mother. She had never been successful at making a blend of Julia and doctors. And how Kern could conceivably do so she didn't know. Julia looked prepared for a battle to the death, as if she knew the subject were going to come up.

"Could you eat some breakfast, darling?" Trisha asked.

"An omelet, if it wouldn't be too much trouble," Mrs. Lowery requested. "No salt—you know, Patricia."

But Kern made it to the refrigerator before she did, scooping out two eggs from a new carton with his left hand. They would have immediately rolled off the counter if she hadn't swooped for them, for he was already bending down to get a bowl. "Tish, you've waited long enough for that coffee. Now just sit down," he ordered flatly.

"It's no problem, Kern," she insisted, but he was already cracking the eggs. The lithe animal grace he carried with him in the woods didn't seem to extend to the kitchen. More than half the eggs slopped over the side of the bowl and the other half dripped stickily from his palm. For an instant he looked at his hand as if shocked he could conceivably make such a mess, and Trisha could not hold back a full-throated chuckle.

"You're not meant to be a lefty, Kern," she chided teasingly and chuckled all over again when he glared at her.

"I've been holding my own in a kitchen for some time."

"Have you?" she said dryly, remembering all too well how expertly acquainted Rhea was with his kitchen.

"Just sit down and have your coffee!"

Well, she was willing, but she watched. The cleaned mushrooms were already on the counter from before. He got out a paring knife, and just as Trisha had the caffeine inches from her lips he sliced through his finger with all the skill of a two-year-old in a china shop. She put down her coffee for the third time, half pushed him to the sink, and turned on the cold-water tap to the point where it splashed back, spraying Kern and Trisha equally. Kern burst out laughing.

"Well, I've never seen anyone so inept in my entire life." Trisha defended herself as she adjusted the water and propelled the cut beneath the spray. "Of all the idiotic . . . when you *know* you can't use your right hand . . ."

"I think the idea is to clean a cut, not drown it."

"And knowing you, all the first-aid supplies are down at the camp!"

"Trisha," he said dryly, "it's nothing. The only reason it hurts is because you're cutting off all the circulation in my wrist."

Both her hands were enclosed tightly on Kern's hand to keep his finger under the water. Her shoulder was half tucked under his, her bottom pressed to his thigh. His face was only inches from hers when she half turned in sudden startled awareness of him. Devilment shone from his gray eyes; his mouth, nearly hidden in the dark beard, was twitching—but there was something else. For a moment she felt caught up in the circle of his arms, and his bandaged wrist lifted to the nape of her neck, chafed and yet seemed to caress the soft skin there. "How surprising—that you're so concerned," he whispered.

She stepped back from him as if burned. "Well, it isn't 'nothing.' It's still bleeding. You need a Band-Aid."

"Do you think there's a remote possibility between the two of you that I could at least have a cup of coffee?" Julia interrupted, with a smug little smile as she surveyed the two of them.

Trisha moved to stir the eggs in the bowl again, but Kern followed, reaching above her, one hand balancing on the curve of her hip. Like hell it was balancing. She jerked away, glaring up at him.

"I was just getting a Band-Aid. If you wouldn't mind putting it on for me—"

"Your mother will do it," Trisha said sharply. What was this? Her specialty was emotional cool. She hadn't felt that particular brand of sheer sexual nervousness around any man since . . . five years ago. It was appalling, and she concentrated totally on Julia's breakfast, finally serving it as she brought her now-cool coffee to the table. Kern and Julia had been talking. Avoiding Kern's eyes, she sat next to Julia, grasping her coffee cup as if subconsciously she was afraid someone would take it away from her. An addict without her fix, she knew coffee would put everything back in perspective again.

". . . so about eleven, I'll take you around the place,

Mother. I would take you earlier, but Trisha insists you see a doctor this morning."

Her jaw dropped, and Julia laid wounded eyes on her. "Patricia, I am perfectly all right! I told you that yesterday. I've had my rest—"

"And you're looking wonderful." Kern lied, seeming completely sympathetic to his mother's cause. "But when Tish made such a fuss this morning I called Ted. At least he's a friend, mother, not some stranger. Having been through a round of doctors after this little accident, I'm beginning to understand how you feel about the medical profession."

"They all want something to be wrong with you," Julia said with an injured tone. "Just so they can keep you coming back—"

Kern nodded. "Always poking needles—"

"You don't know the half of it at your age. You reach sixty and all they talk is angiograms, and the cost..."

Trisha hadn't known Julia had had an angiogram. Julia switched doctors like dresses. If she didn't like the diagnosis, she changed the doctor. It was difficult not to forgive Kern for making her the scapegoat, when his method of extracting information from his mother gleaned more than her coaxing or scolding.

"Well, I've never been overnight in a hospital..." Kern continued.

"But *I* have, Kern. The food is horrible, people poking and prodding all the time. And consultants—now that's another dreadful racket. You can't have just one doctor; an internist won't even talk to you unless there's a heart man there..."

Kern reached for his coffee cup with a casually interested expression toward his mother that didn't fool

Trisha at all. "Well, you don't have to do a thing you don't want to. It's Tish's problem if she wants to hightail it out of here this morning. So you can just stay here with me. I'll be driving back north at the end of August anyway."

Julia nearly choked on her coffee. "Stay, Kern? A few days perhaps, but I have a club meeting on Friday. Trisha, you can surely stay until—"

"Tish said she was leaving this morning, with you or without you . . . unless you saw a doctor this morning," Kern continued sadly. "Actually, I thought I had her all talked into staying a few days, too, Mother, but . . ."

Lord, he was good at it. Trisha marveled, not just at his ability to maneuver his mother. He already had *her* jumpy around him, making his breakfast, taking care of his cuts, now somehow staying longer than she wanted to. He was the same overwhelming Kern. The old Trisha had been lost in that power of his, but it didn't feel quite the same now. She could see what he was doing, for one thing, and more important, she understood why.

"Well, if you'll agree to stay a few days, Patricia," Julia said petulantly. "I must say it's all a mountain for a molehill, but if you really must be so ridiculously obstinate about it . . ."

"I am," she said frankly and turned with an impish smile to Kern. "Just what time is this appointment I insisted on making, Kern?"

"Nine, bright eyes."

What a rogue he was, she thought fleetingly.

4

TED BASSETT'S OFFICE was in a corner of Gatlinburg's hospital complex. Once Trisha had ushered Julia into a private room she was free at least to walk the white-walled corridors, which she did, with increasing anxiety, for more than two hours. She stopped only once to grab a machine cup of coffee that promptly churned in her stomach.

Thoroughly frightened by the long wait, Trisha gave up her pacing finally to lean back against the green-striped wallpaper in the doctor's outer office. When Ted did come out, it was not through the door of the examining room as she expected, but from the main corridor that led to the hospital's admitting wing. Ted took her arm and led her back to his private office.

Tall, lanky, and sandy-haired, Kern's friend had a lazy slow smile and a compassionate sense of humor. "As much as I'd love to send Mrs. Lowery home with you, Trisha, I've decided to tie her to a bed for a good forty-eight hours. Penance mostly. She told one of my nurses to take up sewing because it was certainly her *only* skill with a needle, and the other was scolded for making hypochondriacs out of perfectly healthy people."

Trisha managed a smile, knowing Julia, knowing this gentle man was trying to put her at her ease. "I'd rather simply hear it, please," she said quietly.

Just as quietly, Ted told her. Julia's blood pressure was nearing stroke level. She didn't even pretend to take the medicine prescribed previously for her. She had a heart murmur he was frankly not happy about. His recommendation was a full forty-eight hours of proper rest and medication under controlled conditions—and by controlled he meant that he would prefer no visitors during that time. "And if you know of anything that's bothering her..."

"Not exactly," Trisha said slowly, not wanting to think about the five-year status of her relationship with Julia's son.

"I've only given you my professional opinion, Trisha, and though I've got your mother-in-law installed in a hospital room at the moment, she is certainly of age and not at all convinced she's staying..."

"Oh, she's staying." Trisha stood up, mulling over in her mind everything she had heard. She pulled the strap of her purse to her shoulder as she edged toward the door. "I'll see to Julia, doctor, but I would like to call Kern first if you wouldn't mind my using your telephone."

There was no answer at Kern's. It didn't really matter. There was no question what had to be done, and Trisha had no hesitations about doing it on her own. Getting Julia to the hospital wasn't particularly enjoyable and convincing her to stay would be no fun at all.

It was past noon when Trisha opened the hospital

doors and stepped out into the bright mountain sunshine. Gatlinburg was a crowded little tourist hamlet, packed with shops and restaurants and motels aimed to please the Smoky Mountain visitors. At that moment it seemed a completely foreign place as she traversed the asphalt to her car. The day was sweltering hot, but it was tension that dampened her palms. Julia was ill, really ill or potentially so. What was Kern going to say? That it was her fault? Trisha was the one who had allowed Julia to make the trip, thinking she herself could insure her mother-in-law's every comfort, more than willing to cater to every whim. But if she hadn't driven her, would Julia still have made the journey, she wondered.

The car seat was boiling and a throng of traffic lights prevented any speed that might have cooled the inside. Despite the difficult times, Julia had been good to her over the years, and the idea of something really happening to her felt like a leaden weight in her heart. She had promised Julia she would stay until Thursday afternoon, when she was to be released.

Her mood calmed finally as she escaped the city and Julia's Mercedes began a meandering climb as the road came closer to Kern's. Ted Bassett was his friend and Kern must trust him as a doctor. It seemed she simply had to trust him as well. She could not regret the decision made.

Sun shot through the fleeting bluish mists on the hillsides, piercing colors and scents into the day. The farthest slopes were a velvet green. It was almost a fairy-tale world of lush green peace, of rich scents and sounds. The countryside reached out to her as she drove, just as it had the night before, enfolding her in such a way that she felt herself relax. There was simply nothing else to do until she could talk to Kern.

When she arrived back at the house Kern wasn't there. She parked the small car, leaving ample space for his truck when it returned, and went into the kitchen. It was past one, and she had had nothing but two bites of breakfast since six that morning. Absently she slashed off a wedge of cheese found in the refrigerator and snatched a handful of blueberries, leaning against the back door of the porch as she waited for him.

A rumble of thunder echoed in the west. It was nearly three and there was still no sign of Kern. The storm had been coming in for an hour. Trisha could sense the increasing uneasiness in the air. She watched it from the living room for a time, restless and uneasy herself after two hours of waiting. When the first splashes of rain pattered on the west side of the house she hurried to close the windows where the rain would come in, and put on a fresh pot of coffee. Lightning, stark and silver, suddenly silhouetted the entire west horizon. It was like a low, angry growl building in the skies, accenting the stillness in the house.

She could not stay inside any longer. Where was he? She walked outside to the sheltered back porch, worried eyes peeled for the sight of his truck coming up the narrow mountain lane. Absently she stretched her arm beyond the shelter of the porch. The big drops were oddly warm, almost hot on the sultry afternoon.

At last she heard the sound of the truck engine, and she clattered immediately down the steps to meet it. Her mind was too much on Julia to worry about the rain, though even in those few moments the warm pelter soaked her jersey dress, which clung to her slender figure as she ran to the truck.

Kern stepped out from the vehicle, shouting above

another roar of thunder. "For God's sake, Tish, you're soaking wet! What are you doing out here?"

"Where have you been, Kern? I had to put your mother in the hospital. I tried to call you but you didn't answer, and the doctor seemed to feel—"

"Hey, slow down, bright eyes." His hair was plastered to his skull like a gleaming black helmet, his eyes devil-bright, skimming over her clearly outlined figure in the damp dress. She could feel a flush on her face as she reached up to push back wet hair that drooped in her eyes. "This rain is heaven-sent," he said calmly. "Beyond an occasional shower in the morning, it's been dry as tinder around here for almost three weeks. Forest-fire weather—and if nature wasn't enough to worry about there've been arsonists plaguing the area."

"Arsonists?" Trisha questioned, momentarily diverted from the speech she had carefully prepared on Julia's state of affairs. "Where *have* you been all afternoon?"

"With some of the park service people," he answered. "There's been an outbreak of forest fires this spring. Three last Sunday alone. The best guess is that it's diversion—start a fire here and draw attention away from the location where the thief wants to loot. Or worse yet, some idiots getting their thrills by setting fires . . . Is there some reason we have to discuss this in the middle of a downpour?" he demanded abruptly, his eyes glinting rueful humor.

"It feels good," she said impishly.

"Maybe you haven't turned into such a city girl as you've led me to think," Kern drawled.

"It's just that it was hot, Kern," she said flatly, annoyed by the personal comment. And annoyed that she found herself staring at his chest, outlined clearly through the now-damp shirt, dark hair just beginning to curl at the V of his collar. His jeans were beginning to look molded on him, promoting a clear image of hard, muscled thighs and the virility he had never managed to tame, even in a business suit. He was staring at her just as intently. She knew the rain had washed off her makeup and destroyed the neat coil of chignon. With the sophisticated veneer gone, she could not hide that she'd been almost ridiculously happy to see him.

A ribbon of lightning crackled overhead, and suddenly Kern was pushing her abruptly to the house. "Could you make us a quick cup of coffee, Tish, while I put a few things away?"

"I have to tell you about your mother—"

"In a minute. I've already gathered she's safe and sound in Ted's care. Let's at least talk dry."

She had two cups of coffee in her hand when he came back from his office. Both of them were still undeniably dripping but the warm rain had turned cold inside the house, and Trisha was shivering. He shook his head scoldingly at her, prodding her toward the stairs. "Change clothes, pronto," he ordered.

He followed behind her as she climbed the stairs. "You haven't had any trouble with arsonists here, have you?" she asked worriedly. She knew that the fire towers were always manned in the park. The expensive equipment was maintained to cope with the outbreaks of fire that were inevitable. But no one could control or account for someone who deliberately set a match anywhere on thousands of acres of land.

"Not here. We've got too many people around. But right next to us is the national forest and the wind's never concerned about the property lines. The handful of individual landowners with property bordering the park have gotten together with the park service in a help-each-other sort of program."

She stopped by the door to her room as he kept on striding toward the master bedroom. She frowned when she realized he wasn't going to say any more. And then rather awkwardly she followed him to his door. "How close have the fires been to here?" she asked, and then caught herself up abruptly. It just was not any of her business anymore. Why did she have to remind herself of that? "Never mind about the fires, Kern. I have to tell you about Julia!"

"So tell me."

But the look of the master bedroom silenced her for a moment. It was the first room they had finished a long time ago, a measure, she thought then, of what was important to Kern in a marriage. Wide and long, the room had a thick dark-pumpkin carpet and dark cedar paneling. One stretch of wall was glass, and another streak of lightning illuminated the hills. An Indian print spread in burnt oranges and browns covered the king-sized bed, and a brick fireplace filled one corner. It was a sensual room with the dark wood and rich colors, a room of textures meant to be explored. Her face unconsciously paled in old memories, and when she glanced at Kern it paled further.

He was paying no attention to her. He had already shrugged off his damp shirt and stood with his back to the windows, his powerful frame silhouetted against the darkened room and the mountains in the distance. His chest had a triangle of dark hair, and broad shoulders gleamed in the afternoon's half-light. There was another dark red scar down his side to match the one on his forehead, but this was longer, jagged, and where the pattern of chest hair thinned at the base of his ribs there was the motly color of a healing bruise. A few cuts and scrapes he had said of the accident. She had the insane urge to touch, to soothe; and at the same time the storm outside seemed to have begun inside of her. He was a vibrant sexual animal, standing tall, sure, never self-conscious of his own body. She was suddenly aware he was watching her, as his left hand reached for his belt buckle. "I thought you were going to tell me about mother."

"I am. I . . ." She took a breath. "Your mother has blood-pressure problems, which I knew, and a heart murmur, which I didn't. The doctor wants her to stay in the hospital for at least today and tomorrow, to check her out and give her a few tests. We pick her up Thursday at four." Her voice faded. She was strangely fascinated with his left hand awkwardly trying to work the belt buckle. She realized she wanted to see him; she wanted to see all of him.

His hand lifted from the buckle. "If you're not going to talk, you'd better get out of those clothes. You're shivering like a rabbit, bright eyes."

She turned quickly, suddenly anxious to be out of that room.

"Wait a minute."

She halted, feeling his palm on her shoulder.

"Don't tell me she went meekly into the hospital."

Trisha half turned, hating the awareness in his eyes. Close up, he smelled as fresh and potent as the rain. Inside herself she could feel the danger of the storm. It was absurd. She had to stop this. "You know your mother, Kern," Trisha said curtly. "It was fifty strokes of the lash, the threat of boiling oil, and the promise I would never again vote liberal as long as I lived—and all that done on bended knees."

He chuckled. "You don't have to tell me that, Tish. I've been trying to get her into the hospital for three years. She's always claiming to have just been to a doctor and come out 'clean.' It took both of us this morning, though if you want me to apologize for making you the scapegoat—"

"It worked, Kern. That's all that matters."

"Do you want to go see her tonight in the hospital?"

"No visitors, the doctors said. I—what are you doing?"

His right palm rested at the nape of her neck, and she could feel an odd warmth flow through her like liquid fire as the fingers of his other hand slowly started to wrestle with the first button of her dress. The heel of his hand rested on the crest of her breast like a caress. "Don't," she said quickly, and jerked away from him, hurrying down the hall into her own room.

She half closed the door and hurried out of the damp dress, her fingers fumbling awkwardly. What *is* the matter with you, she asked herself furiously. She hung the damp dress on a hanger and hooked it on the shower stall to dry. Shivering almost violently, she hurriedly slipped on the ivory pants and blouse from yesterday. It was all she had to wear. The pins were half falling from her hair and she removed the rest, snatching a brush after she'd toweled away most of the moisture.

"Are those really all the clothes you brought with you?"

Trisha half turned to see Kern at the door, a navy shirt over tan pants accenting his long legs and broad-shouldered figure. "Yes," she told him flatly.

"You really weren't planning on even seeing me if you could help it, were you, Tish?"

There was more than a hint of harshness in his voice. She set down the brush. Her hair was simply brushed back from her forehead, a style that accented the proud line of her bone structure. "No," she admitted quietly. "And now I've promised your mother I'll stay until Thursday. Even if I hadn't promised, I couldn't leave now without knowing how she was. I'm sure it will be awkward for you with Rhea. I'll just move to a motel, Kern—"

"Rhea? What does she have to do with anything?"

Trisha rearranged the collar on her blouse and aimed for the door. She favored Kern with a cool glance she was frankly proud of. "I wasn't criticizing," she said evenly. "Or trying to pry."

His jaw tightened. As she walked down the stairs, she sensed that Kern was leashing whatever he was feeling, whatever he might have wanted to say. "You'll stay here. And if that's all the clothes you've got with you, the next thing on the agenda is something for you to wear."

"I don't need anything."

"The two outfits you brought with you won't last five minutes outside in this country. Or are you planning on being cooped up indoors for two days like you used to?"

She considered how very nice it would have been to be a man on a football team pitted against Kern in his college days. One of those fellows who butted a hard-helmeted head directly into the opposition's stomach.

"All right," she said testily. "I'll go out and get a pair of jeans."

"How . . . sensible. I'll go with you."

Her eyes flashed exasperation with him. "Thanks, but no thanks. I pick out my own clothes these days, Kern, imagine that!"

"It's raining like hell. I can't get any work done in this weather, so we'll go out to dinner afterwards." Irritatingly calm gray eyes surveyed her increasingly troubled ones. "All upset, bright eyes," he chided scoldingly. "When you know damn well you didn't bring any more money than you needed for the trip home. So the clothes will be on me, Tish, and you're even driving: I had enough of one-handed driving this afternoon. Surely that's enough to rate a smile?"

They raced to the Mercedes in the pelting rain. Breathless, they both slammed their doors against the storm at the same time and Trisha reached for her key. Flipping back her hair from her cheeks she turned on the wipers and lights, and backed out of the driveway. There was a tension locked inside the car's small interior that made the Mercedes feel like a cage. It was a tension that had been building from the moment she'd arrived. Trisha had had enough of it.

"Kern?"

He arched a questioning eyebrow in her direction. Both of her hands stayed firmly on the wheel, her eyes boring straight ahead. "Just stop it, would you?"

"Stop what?"

"All of it . . . your telling people I'm your wife . . . your kissing me . . . the way you look at me. You couldn't conceivably have been glad to see me, Kern, and I didn't expect you to be." She hesitated, biting her lip as she reached to turn on the defroster. "So you're stuck with me and maybe we both have to make the best of it for a short time. But I've felt like... you've been playing some game with me."

He didn't answer, simply stared at her as she continued to drive. By the time they stopped at a shopping center in Gatlinburg, Trisha was a blend of chin-up pride and anxiety. She had spoken what she felt. That was no crime. Yet no one accused Kern of playing games. He radiated integrity from the core. Which was all the more confusing...

Inside the store, Kern was without question the strangest patron there, a tall, bearded giant threading through size five's with the same interest he took in doing anything new—at least once. It took Trisha less than five minutes to find what she wanted and cart it to the dressing room. The tan designer jeans fit perfectly, a match for the dark blonde of her hair. A silky pale-blue blouse with tan at the gathered-yolk bodice matched it. Slipping her cream pantsuit back on, she was soon out of the dressing room carrying her potential purchases over one arm.

And Kern was standing right there, with potential purchases over his arm and a salesgirl hovering with hopeful enthusiasm just behind him. "Now don't get snippy," he said the moment he saw the expression on her face. "One pair of jeans may very well do for the morning, but afternoons are hot; you may need something to swim in, and since it's my money I don't see why you should care anyway."

But it was precisely because it *was* his money that she did care. Why he even wanted to buy her the mound of clothes didn't really register. The feeling of owing him for one outfit already grated, and the pile of fabric was almost enough to induce a ridiculous sense of panic that she couldn't quite explain. Worse than that was the inalterable feeling that he wanted her to bicker, wanted her to show that she was afraid of... what? Staying? Her lips pressed in a tight smile, Trisha handed the slacks and blouse she had chosen to the waiting salesgirl and turned smoothly to his pile.

"It's very nice of you, Kern, I'm sure." Her tone said that she thought differently, as she took the bright orange outfit from his arm and laid it on the counter. "That's really a color for a brunette. This one, the manufacturer specializes in short waists and I'm long-waisted, I'm afraid. I like this one, I really do, but I've never been able to wear that style blouse..." The pile on the counter kept mounting. Her polite, cheerful tone never altered until she came to the last of the clothes and then she faltered, a blush stealing onto her cheeks as she picked up the lemon open-weave bikini with two fingers and tossed it on top of the pile.

"You always look good in yellow." His eyes dared her to name her excuse. With a glance intended to wither steel, she stalked out of the store.

He met her outside all too soon with her bag in his hand. His full-throated chuckle vibrated between them as he grabbed her arm and they raced again through the rain to the car. "You're still a prude, Tish," he teased as she slammed the door on her side.

She pulled out in traffic in the direction of the restaurant he'd named, her chin stiffly in the air. "That isn't fair. The only reason I don't wear that kind of thing is because I don't have the figure for it."

"And that's the most ridiculous thing I've ever heard. Sexy's the way the whole shape's put together, not just a pair of pendulous breasts—"

"I don't believe this conversation!"

"I don't believe you just went through a red light."

Her eyes flickered anxiously to the rearview mirror, and he burst into laughter when she shot back daggers at him. It was the first red light she had ever run in her life.

"I wouldn't have wanted you to wear it in public anyway," he consoled.

"If I had wanted to wear something like that, I would have worn it whether or not you or anyone else approved," she said snappishly.

"I see. You're going to argue no matter what I say." He sighed. "And I suppose the next thing you're probably thinking to do is to go back to the shop to get it. Just to prove I'm wrong."

He had an unforgivable understanding of her exact frame of mind. Belatedly she realized that Kern had not worried about the entire pile of clothes. It was that little lemon confection at the bottom that he had staged to unsettle her. Or was it to find out if she really was the same prudish, self-conscious little nitwit she used to be? Somehow, it mattered that he believed she had changed, really changed. It was a question of pride.

"You misunderstand, Kern," she said more calmly. "I have no real objections to the suit—only to wearing something like it in a public place, like the swimming hole by the camp where there are so many strangers. Of course if you consider that prudish, I have to admit . . ." She shrugged carelessly, and followed his motioning hand to the parking-lot entrance near the restaurant.

"But one-on-one is just fine, is that it, Tish?"

His voice told of his displeasure, and for no reason as far as she could surmise. She sighed, giving up. She did not understand the man or his attitude. But she was exceedingly hungry.

The restaurant was new to her. Huge from the outside, from within it was divided into at least half-a-dozen smaller dining rooms. Neither of them were dressed formally, but Kern chose to lead them to a small, hushed room in the back. Blood-red linen tablecloths and flickering candles graced each table. The menus were impressively two-feet long, and Trisha promptly hid behind hers.

For a few minutes they were both quiet, and in spite of herself Trisha found that she was relaxing. Perhaps it was the pent-up sigh from the other side of the table that signaled a truce, and finally Kern spoke from behind his menu. "Are we going polite or are we going for fingers, Tish?"

She could not help a smile as she peered around the menu. "Fingers."

"Fine." He closed the menu, took hers from her, and set them aside. "You're having frog legs and I'm having lobster. There's really no need to look at the rest of the list." He paused, a small flame in his eyes from the reflection of the candle. "I'm already picturing you in one of those big bibs..."

"And I'm picturing you with your beard, managing lobster dripping with butter," she quipped back.

They both ate without a lot of talk, devouring their favorite delicacies as if starved. A small decanter of white wine was placed between them and was nearly empty by the time they finished. There was the sound of laughter and muted conversation from the other rooms, but the small dining area they claimed was virtually empty except for the two of them. When the bibs and bones and shells and debris from their meal were removed, the dark-coated waiter served coffee, and they both leaned back in their chairs, replete to the point of a lazy kind of tiredness.

"Ready?" Kern asked finally, and she nodded. His arm brushed the small of her back as they walked from the restaurant, and when they reached the car Kern slipped into the driver's seat. Taking control, she thought fleetingly, the way Kern found it hard not to take control of a setting. At the moment it just didn't matter. She was too full, feeling perfectly lazy, to let anything matter. She slipped down in the passenger seat, resting her head against the back, half closing her eyes as he started the engine. The torrential rain had finally stopped and night had descended on the valley. They were through the flashing neon lights of the town in minutes and back on the mountain road that invoked an intense, peaceful quiet.

"I haven't seen you wear the sling since yesterday," she commented idly.

Kern smiled ruefully. "Ted told me the wrist would have healed a week ago if I'd just done what he told me. The sling was a penance that afternoon for overdoing it. Bothered by my driving, Tish?"

"Of course not," she said sleepily. "You drove the truck earlier, Kern. Besides, you wouldn't take the wheel if you couldn't handle it."

He glanced at her. "Blind trust used to be your speciality," he chided.

She looked back at him, and then away, silent the rest of the half-hour drive. Blind trust had been the instinct from the moment she met him, she couldn't deny it. Though, thank God, she wasn't naive any longer. But that trust, she realized, was still there. She did trust Kern and his integrity. She couldn't really say the same for anyone else she'd ever known in her life.

On the way up the long drive to his place, Kern turned the car midway, taking a narrow gravel road she was unfamiliar with. "Where?" she asked.

"To walk off a bit of dinner, if you don't mind."

"I...no." She stepped out of the car stiffly, aware of Kern and the fact that they were alone. Somehow in all the worry over Julia she had failed to remind herself that staying at his place meant staying *alone* with him for the two nights.

"This way."

He helped her over a rocky patch, and then his hand fell away, leaving her to set her own pace ahead of him. Trees rustled on her left, but the path followed a stream on the right, a gurgling rush of silver in the moonlight, a sprinkling of stars overhead reflected in the water. Wildflowers crouched low all around the banks, a sweet, potent, night-rich scent after the rain.

They walked without talking. The darkness made for a meandering pace, but it was not pitch black. The rain had cooled the sultry heat of the day, just a faint warm breeze rippling the stream. When she tired of walking, she wandered to a low flat rock that jutted over the water and perched on it with her legs crossed, bending to look in the stream.

Kern stopped just behind her, leaning back against the rough-barked surface of a hickory tree in the shadow. She glanced back once, all too aware of him, but he seemed no more inclined to talk than she did. Every limb gradually relaxed as she simply stared out over the water, absorbing the scene. The restfulness was so different from the city life she'd adjusted to—the life she had convinced herself was all and exactly what she wanted. But the convincing had taken a long time.

Finally she stood back up and dusted off her pants. She looked again to Kern. He hadn't moved. His eyes had a gleam in the dusty shadows beneath the tree. She felt uneasy.

"You accused me of playing with you before."

She nodded, pushing her hair back where the breeze was trying to curl it to her cheeks.

"I knew we'd see each other again sometime, Tish. For the first year after you left, I probably would have slammed the door in your face if you had come back." He stepped out from the shadows toward her, and she dug her hands in her pockets. "It took a long time to accept failure. I blamed you first and then me . . . and then no one. There was certainly no way to take back those six months, was there?"

She shook her head, and he added quietly, "You were very young, Tish. I knew sooner or later I would want to know what you would be like when you grew up."

She took a breath, still staring at him. "I kept expecting you to ask for a divorce."

"I want children. If I'd found someone along the way I'd wanted to have children with, I would have gotten a divorce. Until then, it didn't really matter."

He might as well have said that she didn't matter, beyond sheer curiosity as to what had happened to her. She felt an unexpected curl of pain in her stomach.

"And you have grown up, Tish."

His tone was soft, and she shook her head when he started toward her. She knew why he was coming, what he wanted, but the mesmerizing hold in his eyes was difficult to look away from. Her hands trembled just from the brush of those eyes on her soft skin.

"I'm not asking or even suggesting fresh starts, Tish. I don't even know who you are anymore, but I know damn well there's something that you're not leaving here again without . . . You can feel it . . . I can feel it every time I come near you."

"No. There's nothing, Kern, there's . . ."

She put her hands in front of her as if that would be enough to push him away. A shudder whispered through her from fingers to toes as his lips molded hers, gently, insistently persuasive. His fingers caressed her face and throat, like they had done the first time when she had fallen in love with him. His tongue flicked across her teeth and her lips parted for him, her eyes closed half in dread, half in anticipation. The leashed lovemaking was Kern's sweetness, but unleashed there were old nightmares . . .

"Put your arms around my neck, Tish," he whispered. "You did it last night."

"No. Please, Kern. This is all wrong . . ."

"Just for a moment," he coaxed. He drew her slim hands up himself, placing them around his neck, and his lips softly brushed her eyes closed again, brushed a sweet seductive warmth down the side of her face and neck. Her fingers crumpled in the rough thick texture of his hair. The need to hold on was there. She felt his strength beneath her fingertips, his flesh so warm, so responsive to her lightest touch. The earthy male scent of him enfolded her like a sweet drug she could not escape from, suddenly uncertain if she even wanted to. The panic that should have been mounting didn't. She felt her breasts stiffen against his heartbeat, felt her thighs yield to the pressure of his own. So fierce was the growing awareness that she suddenly felt desperate for air but he would give her none. Her throat arched back as his mouth pressed on hers, a pressure that ached bruisingly against her lips, a pressure that echoed in the tightening spasms at the pit of her stomach.

She knew better. Kern had not spoken of a renewal of their marriage and there was no way she would ever surrender again to that old feeling of being on trial, risk that sense of inadequacy as a woman that had almost destroyed her. But for a sweet shivering moment that seemed exactly the point. It was over with Kern, so there was really nothing left to lose.

She molded her body to Kern's, pressing her soft fluid thighs to his sinewed hardness, as her tongue parried with his. Her hands kneaded the nape of his neck, his shoulders, the long, endlessly long stretch of his back to his waist. Kern matched fire with fire, his lips leaving hers only for breath before his teeth grazed her neck as if he were hungry for her taste. His bandaged wrist chafed the tender skin of her ribs under her blouse, summoning other fires. A work-roughened palm was impatient with the slip of bra, until it found the silky pale orb of flesh beneath, until the nipple tightened and swelled and strained beneath it.

Something burst inside Trisha, a Pandora's box of desire and need suddenly freed. She could not touch him enough. Her hands roamed feverishly beneath his shirt, up and down his sides and back, instinctively careful of the scar.

"Lord, I want you, Tish. I've always wanted you," he murmured huskily.

She felt like crying. The wildness inside her would not stop building. She wanted to possess him and to be taken as she had never wanted to be taken before, not caring for past, present, future, not caring about the night or the rocky terrain or the dampness.

It was all so easy. Kern was urging her down, his hands and eyes compelling her to lay beneath him. But his eyes left hers for just that moment, closing when he tried to bend where his ribs would not yet allow him to bend, his right wrist taking weight it was not yet ready to take. In the moonlight she saw his face contort in sudden unwilling pain, and she froze.

The next thing she knew she was running. Stumbling on the rock-rough ground, tears blinding her, she made her hands try to put together blouse and bra and hair. Her chest was heaving in the chill night air. Shame, pride, memories . . . the internal ache was as sharp as a knife edge in her side when she finally reached the car and stopped, leaning weakly on the hood. She felt like fragments inside. From wanton to cold made no sense. Not to respond when he had loved her, to go on fire when there was only chemistry and no future. To completely forget that the man was hurt and in no shape for violent lovemaking, to forget every ounce of self-respect that had put her back together in those long years . . .

"Get in," Kern ordered.

His shirt was flapping open. His eyes like icy coals as he opened the car door, he snatched at her arm and all but shoved her across to the passenger seat. The door slammed like a reverberating echo in her ear and Trisha huddled in the seat, eyes suddenly dry. His tall figure crossing in front of the car reflected a cold-hard fury that frightened her. When he got inside he just looked at her tousled features long and hard and then started the engine.

They were at his place in minutes. The single light left on in the kitchen made a lonely circle of welcome on the grass outside. Trisha reached quickly for the door handle, but Kern's arm shot across, pinning her.

"Tell me you intended to leave, just when—" he said harshly.

She shook her head mutely, and his grip impercep- tively lightened.

"I told you I wondered what would happen when you grew up, Tish. Now I wonder how many men were part of that transition. You never took fire like that before. How many?" He grated. "How many men have you slept with in the past five years?"

She was frightened still, his eyes intense, smoldering anger inches from hers. She knew he wouldn't believe the truth. It struck her as almost hysterically funny to think of telling him after what just happened that she had almost led a nun's life, that she had accepted finally that she was simply emotionless in bed. She didn't understand yet why she had responded to him after all these years. And, if it weren't for the mortifying confusion and em- barrassment she felt inside, the bitter scald of tears held barely in check, she would not believe she had indeed responded.

"Never mind." His jaw was taut, but the longer he looked at her fragile feminine features contorted by an- guish, the more the flame of rage in his eyes lessened. "We're not done, Tish. It's going to happen, and you damn well know it as well as I do. With us there's only one ending or beginning, because of the way it was."

She breathed out no.

He wasn't listening. "You run this time and I'll find you. Don't even try it."

She opened the car door and escaped. The kitchen door was unlocked and she ran through, past the living room and hall, up the stairs. In seconds she was leaning against the closed door of her bedroom, fighting to stop the flow of hot tears.

Sex was all he had been talking about, not love. He felt no love after all this time? *Why should he* was the silent cry inside.

She moved forward, removing her clothes in the darkness. The urge was to pack and flee. The urge was to forget Julia. But unfortunately she simply could not forget. Her pulse finally calmed. She was not running again. It was time for action, time to get them both out of their limbo of a marriage. Five years past time.

But she could never face going to bed with Kern again. Even after tonight, she didn't trust herself. She would freeze and fail him. The last time, she had put herself back together. She knew she wouldn't be able to do it again. Not again . . .

5

TRISHA DID NOT wake until nine, a late hour in this household, so she was not surprised to find the house empty and no sign of Kern when she went downtairs. Dressed in the new jeans and shirt, with a battered pair of tennis shoes she'd remembered to throw into her suitcase, she gulped down half a cup of coffee and carted a sweet roll outside with her.

She was determined to work herself into a better frame of mind. Last night she had slept long and hard, but dreams had haunted her. Kern's lovemaking had been rapturously consummated in one dream; yet in another he had thrown the name of tease at her, which churned like pain inside. In a third dream he had repeated over and over, "There's only one way it can end for us, Tish. In bed. I can get you out of my system so easily if I see once and for all how cold and ungiving a woman you are!"

Daylight had come as a relief. She felt a need to do something physical to distract her from the increasing confusion she felt around Kern. Brushing crumbs off her hands from the roll, she shoved her hands in her back pockets and walked.

Kern's land was a unique blend of landscapes. At the highest level was the spruce and fir forest, dense and abundant with berries at this time of the year, trillium sometimes blanketing a long stretch of forest floor. Some of the most spectacular waterfalls were above those areas he kept private, one of which she knew was uniquely special to any place on earth, yet it was not where she headed.

Below the fir-tipped peaks was the kind of land the campers came for, the cove-hardwood forest the region was famous for. It was magical to walk through. The huge tree trunks, some so wide four or five men couldn't span their arms around them, stretched to the sky, forming leafy umbrellas high above her head. Yellow poplar, oak, basswood, hemlock—she remembered only a few of the names. Sunlight dappled down in long dusty streaks, shining on dogwood and rhododendron and an incredible number of wildflowers that only flourished in this protected area. Soft mosses covering the rich dark earth felt spongy beneath her feet.

An unusual wistfulness touched her expression as she walked. The city was her life now. She had roots established and a frenetically paced job that usually suited her well. But unwillingly, she could too easily remember that it wasn't a cement-and-computer world where she'd wanted to raise her children, but here, with nature's values and nature's laws.

A hot whispering breeze brushed against her cheeks as she continued on, trailing a sprawling pattern of delicate white mountain laurel that bordered the path. Half an hour later she glimpsed the roof of Kern's horse barn, and a wry smile touched her lips. Out of simple curiosity she headed that way. It was very dark inside, and the smells seemed doubly pervasive because of it. Trisha loved the smell of leather that was well cared for and recently polished, fresh hay, and the scent of the horses themselves.

She noticed that two stalls were empty and suspected that either Kern or Jack had rented the horses out to campers. One horse stomped his feet at the sound of the stranger entering; another let out a plaintive whinny, bored after yesterday's rain and inactivity. She stroked the silky necks as she ambled by. Four of the horses she'd never seen before, but of course Kern would have expanded his stock in five years.

"Would you ride with me?"

Trisha whirled, startled by the sudden tiny voice that seemed to come from nowhere. "Hello," she offered cheerfully to the pigtailed little blonde dejectedly leaning against the stable door. She recognized the child from breakfast the day before. "It's Georgia, isn't it?"

The child nodded. "Would you go for a little ride with me?" she requested again. "My mom's sick, and my dad promised but now he can't. I can ride real good, but no one will let me go alone."

Trisha crouched down to be more on a level with the big sad eyes. "Oh, I'd love to, honey, but I'm not very good with horses. I wouldn't even know how to saddle one."

The big blue eyes fluttered wide with hope. "You don't need saddles. You just put on a big blanket. We could just go for a little while. Mr. Jack'll say okay, and so will my daddy. Please? Oh, please?"

"Honey, I just can't..."

One huge crystal of a tear formed in the child's eye and slowly dribbled down her cheek. Trisha sighed. The first time she had gotten on a horse she had set off at an instant gallop and all too soon found herself head over heels, rolling on the ground. Her relationship with horses from then on had been never to travel in the direction of the stables without sugar, carrots or apples, all of which she was willing to deliver with crooning words and petting, and all from the other side of the wooden gates.

Georgia's mother was still in her nightgown and nursing a cold. Her father was making tea for his wife. Trisha went into humorous detail as to her utter lack of experience with horses, her proven lack of control over them, and the more relevant fact that Georgia was their only daughter. The Shearers were clearly more interested—and grateful—in the idea of a baby-sitter.

And Jack proved equally helpful, bustling promptly ahead of them to put the reins and blanket on a huge roan at the far end of the stables. "Kern already told me to give you any help you wanted if you wandered down here. I thought he said for sure you wouldn't be near the horses, but it doesn't matter. Mildred's just a lamb, and I'll show you a good easy trail to follow. You won't run into any trouble. If you're worried at all, though, I'll get a mount and go with you. Kern said—"

"No, thank you," Trisha said firmly, aware of the blonde's admiring look. She grinned. "Some humiliations are better faced alone. A lamb, you say?"

"Really, she's very gentle."

It was not as if she had other plans for the morning, and a short trip around the campgrounds wasn't going to kill her. Georgia comfortably vaulted in front like a pro, and Jack helped Trisha slide on just behind her.

Three hours later Trisha snail-paced the walk to Kern's with a gamboling Georgia at her side, seeking lunch. Hurrying was not the order of the day. Unconsciously she stiffened still further at the sight of Kern at the door, his arms folded across his chest as if he had been waiting. His eyes narrowed only momentarily on the child and then rested on Trisha, who was making a momumental effort to walk normally.

"I was about to send out a search party for you. There was a time you wouldn't go a quarter mile off the trail on your own, bright eyes; and in this country, if you haven't forgotten, one leaves word before just taking off for hours at a time."

"It never occurred to me that you would be worried," she answered honestly, not at all pleased that just looking at him was enough to promote an image of last night, of steel-gray eyes softened in passion. She swept past him to the cool bright kitchen with the child in hand, all too aware he was radiating both impatience and exasperation. "I'm sorry, Kern. I knew you were busy and I never planned on being in your way. Jack knew where we were. Have you had lunch?"

"I would have, but I kept expecting you to come in. Rhea had been coming over to fix meals, but somehow she's under the impression that she's not wanted here for the moment. I wonder who could conceivably have given her that idea."

It didn't seem particularly wise to answer that. She ran a quick brush through her hair and washed her hands in the bathroom, returning to the kitchen to make sandwiches, with Georgia perched on the counter next to her. It was Georgia who put cheese, meat, and lettuce to the bread slices. The first finished product, wobbly though it was, was presented proudly to "Mr. Kern," who now sat in a kitchen chair, watching both of them.

"I've never been fond of bolo—" Kern started to say, and was quelled at the pride in the five-year-old's eyes.

Trisha was ridiculously proud of him for rallying. "Thank you, honey," he told her. The child beamed. "Have you been with Trisha all morning?"

Georgia nodded shyly.

"Then would you mind telling me, honey, where the hell—"

"Kern!"

"Where the two of you have been for the last four hours?" he amended.

Georgia's sandwiches were decorated and cut to look like faces, raisins for eyes and carrot curls for smiles. The child sat next to Kern. Trisha had no intention of sitting anywhere. Ever. In the next life there were be no horses, certainly not bony ones. She munched as she continued working, slicing and paring vegetables; there was enough time to make a decent soup for Mrs. Shearer's evening meal.

"We've been riding," Georgia said shyly.

"Have you?" Kern said, as if he were properly impressed. His glance at Trisha reminded her that he knew very well her feeling for horses.

"T'sha rode behind me," Georgia explained seriously. "We rode all over the whole mountains. Mildred didn't want to go home. I didn't either. And Daddy said T'sha could have me all day. I didn't even fall off once."

"And T'sha?" Kern prompted with equal gravity.

"We were going up this huge mountain and T'sha slid off his back. It took ages and ages to get her back on again."

"Did it now?"

"We picked berries," Georgia continued, with growing confidence in the tall, fierce-looking man who seemed remarkably interested in her morning. "Wild berries. And

Mildred ran away. Boy, can she go! I helped T'sha catch her."

Trisha burst out laughing. "Some help! I did the running and you called out between mouthfuls of berries." She swiped at Georgia's face, then at the counter and table, clearing up swiftly and efficiently. She resisted the urge to wipe off Kern's lazy grin as well.

"I'm beginning to get the feeling there's a reason you're not sitting down for your lunch, Tish," Kern drawled.

"Are you?"

"Could I touch your beard?" Georgia requested. "I've never touched a beard."

His eyebrows raised slightly at the request, but he obligingly bent down.

"Kind of scratchy," Georgia judged.

"I can't shave with my left hand," he said as justification. "But in another day or so—"

"Oh, keep it, Kern," Trisha said impulsively, and then could have bitten her tongue. What was it to her if he were clean-shaven or bearded, and the slate-gray eyes were suddenly on her like a floodlight. "Or shave it off. As you like, of course," she added with careful indifference.

"So you suddenly have a liking for beards, do you?"

"No, I—"

"Suddenly you put together an old-fashioned mountain breakfast in fifteen minutes flat. I see you've got your makeup off and a smudge of dirt on your jeans. And up on a horse again..." He shook his head in mocking disbelief, but his eyes held a gleam in them that reflected last night's memories. Those things were not the only things that had changed in Trisha. "If you don't watch it, you might just fall in love with the mountain life all over again, Tish—"

"You must not have been listening to the story," she said stiffly. "If you needed proof I'm a city girl, Kern, all you had to do was hear how I fell off the most placid 'lamb' in your stables!"

Kern stood up, stretching lazily. "Would you like a good rubdown, bright eyes? If you're complaining of stiff muscles..." His eyes took in the fit of her snug pair of jeans, the way it would all fit together without the pair of jeans. Unwillingly Trisha could feel a faint color escape to her cheeks, imagining, as he meant her to, his palms intimately working on...muscles.

"There's no need," she said crisply. "Besides, right after I finish here I'm taking Georgia's mother some soup. She isn't feeling well, and after that—"

After that she'd taken one look at the camp's log-cabin headquarters, and decided to make it the afternoon's project. She had to have something to do with herself for two days, and the need for the cleanup there was a direct measure of Kern's inability to get around since his accident. Jack certainly hadn't objected to the idea; he had all but thrown his arms around her at the offer to reorganize the chaos of files and first-aid supplies and camping equipment.

"Somehow I'm not surprised you managed to make arrangements to be away from here for the afternoon," Kern said dryly. "I thought you'd choose shopping, though, Tish. It's a much farther distance to town." He waited, but she offered no reply. "Rhea's invited the two of us over for dinner at seven."

Trisha turned from the door where Georgia was already headed out, her back suddenly stiff. "Well, you go, of course," she said casually. "I don't think I will, Kern, by then I'll be tired."

He was silent for a moment, and she looked back at him, unable to read the oddly disturbed look in his eyes. "That's what you want, Tish?" he said deliberately.

"I—yes, of course it is." To think of Kern with another woman . . . but of course it was the only answer she could give. She was not part of his life anymore; he wasn't even asking her to be part of his life again. He was only asking her to sleep with him, and she had to be certain he understood she wasn't interested.

It was past nine. About a dozen people were stretched lazily out around the campfire, all of them more or less in the same condition: grubby, sleepy, and sated from the community dinner cooked on the fire not an hour before. Trisha had a half-full can of beer in her hand— she never drank beer—and her tousled blonde head and shoulders were slumped against a huge old log, with Jack on one side of her and little Georgia on the other. She surveyed her stretched-out legs and the absolutely filthy appearance of her jeans with rueful amusement, half listening to the lazy conversations around her. Jack had just put down an old country fiddle that seemed to know all the old Appalachian hill songs, and she was still humming a few in her brain, too tired even to put on her shoes.

"It was a bear and her two cubs, I swear it was . . . you've never seen anyone run so fast in your entire life . . ."

"The trout were just jumping for the bait . . ."

The stories were getting better as the hour was getting later. The smoke from the fire curled in a lazy spiral straight up the cloak of trees surrounding them, making a natural tepee. The night was sleepy warm, and she could hear the hooting of an owl in the distance.

"What I'd give for a life like this all the time," a short, stoop-shouldered man murmured from the distance. "Hey, Jack, what do you have to do around here to buy a piece of ground?"

Jack stirred, edging up to a sitting position beside Trisha. "The way I understand it, there isn't any land for sale around the Smokies. The government gets first shot, unless it's an issue of direct inheritance. It was Kern's grandfather who willed this to him, as I understand it." He looked to Trisha for confirmation, who simply nodded, her eyes half closed as she stared into the fire.

"I just read the park has some 516,000 acres. I wouldn't think anybody'd need more than that," someone else said.

"Well, from here, we can't protect enough land like this," came another lazy voice from the far reaches of the fire. "I've been to the Rockies and I've been to the Tetons. Each mountain area's got its own flavor—this one isn't the grandeur, it's the richness. You just can't get tired of it; there's more different colors of green than an artist could come up with; there's the change in seasons and no end to the wildlife. I keep wondering how God even came up with it . . ."

Smiling, Trisha half sat up, curling up her knees and resting her arms across them. Her soft-spoken voice seemed part of the night, gentle, warm, and sensual. "There's a Cherokee legend about how these mountains came into being. The Indians say that at the beginning of the world everything lived in the sky, all the animals and the people. The world was just an ocean, no land, but unfortunately it got to be crowded up there in the sky, so the Cherokees sent down a little water beetle just to check out the possibilities. Well, the beetle dove to the bottom of the water and brought up mud and more mud, and finally that mud burgeoned up to form some land. But it was still too soft for anyone to live on, so the people sent down a giant buzzard to find a dry spot, but he became tired about the time he was over what was to be Cherokee country. His wings were flapping when he sunk down on the land, and all that flapping dried the mud in the pattern of mountains and valleys . . ."

"*These* mountains and valleys, they say." Kern's voice vibrated low as he wended his way through the lazy pairs of legs to get to her side. Through a chorus of greetings he seemed to be looking only at her, and before she was even aware of it, Jack had obligingly moved and made a place for him next to Trisha. Long, jeaned legs suddenly stretched out next to her. An afternoon and evening of Jack's subtle admiration invoked none of the disturbing sensations that Kern's presence instantly did. Ebony hair and beard, ebony eyes by firelight—he was the pirate who savored his treasure, this land and its richness. Savored, protected, cherished, would kill to keep, she thought whimsically.

"Tish used to love the old Cherokee legends. Has she told you about the Little People yet? They're the keepers of history to the Cherokee, the spirits who come out only at night to share the legends and songs that are too old for any man to remember."

Helplessly she found herself turning to look at him. His deep voice was droning out stories for the others, but his eyes captured hers. For a long unbroken moment there were only two of them, and Kern was the scarred pirate, with a physical power no man could match and a devil fire in his eyes when he looked at her. And for that moment she was his golden treasure, fragile, unable to deny his right to take and hold—and keep. The image held for as long as he stared at her, so strong that she could feel the change in her heartbeat, as real as the night wind that touched her skin. Answering someone's question, he turned away, and she shivered suddenly in the darkness.

"One of those Cherokee spirits just walk over your grave, Trisha?" asked the woman, chuckling, on the other side of Georgia.

"Some ghosts just refuse to rest," Trisha admitted, and with an uneasy little laugh brought her attention deliberately back to the group.

With her just-washed hair turbaned in a towel, Trisha surveyed the meager contents of her traveling wardrobe with irritation. The navy dress had a spot; the cream outfit had been worn twice; the jeans and shirt were filthy; and she'd been wearing the nightgown for five days straight. A long hike was what she'd had in mind for the day, with a grandfatherly man named Edwards she'd met the night before at the camp, a regular visitor of Kern's. As she scooped up the clothes in one hand and carefully wielded her coffee cup with the other, she told herself that with luck she'd have the washing chore done in an hour and have the rest of the day free until four, when she and Kern had to pick up Julia.

As she stepped into the hall with her hands full, the towel she'd been wearing slipped, and by the time she'd taken three more steps it had evidently decided it was happiest in the floor. Automatically her eyes darted up, but there wasn't a soul in the house, since Kern had left more than an hour before in the truck. With an irritated sigh she set everything on the floor, wandered determinedly back to Kern's room, and drew out an old, frayed long-sleeved shirt of his from the back of the closet. The yellow fabric fit predictably, an exercise in drowning. All that identified her feminine status disappeared, and it took five impatient rolls of each cuff just to rediscover her hands.

Adding a hairbrush to the pile on the floor, she snatched it all back up and carted it downstairs. Beyond the bedroom where Julia had stayed was Kern's office study, Beyond that was a utility room, with washing machine and dryer and lemon-painted wall-to-ceiling cupboards for storage. Trisha put the washer setting on cool and gentle, pretreated the stains on the jeans, and then leaned back as the machine filled, absently working the brush through her hair. A large low window made it a pleasant room to be in, utility status or not. Budding azaleas burgeoned over the windowsills; the mossy lawn just outside was lush and emerald, sloping gently to the woods. A pair of woodpeckers were busy trying to peck insects from the bark of a huge old mountain maple, and a red squirrel was perched paws-up in the middle of the lawn, scolding the world in general about nothing in particular. Trisha smiled in amusement; "boomers," the locals labeled the squirrels, for they never ceased their chattering.

From the distance in the woods she caught the soft reflection of a pair of eyes. A white-tailed deer stepped one foot from the safety of cover to the open, civilized carpet of lawn, changed his mind, and bolted with that coltish awkward leap that was a blend of grace and timidity so common in the breed. The red squirrel suddenly hopped after him—at last finding someone to listen? Chuckling, Trisha stretched lazily and took her coffee cup for a refill to the kitchen. It was at least twenty minutes before she needed to do anything else.

Her barefoot step was quick and quiet past Kern's office, and then she backed up unconsciously with a startled frown. The room was new to her, and she'd made a point of not intruding near it since she'd been there. Teak paneling and a dark Oriental carpet reminded her very much of Kern's office in Detroit, shut off from sights and sounds, the way he liked to work.

The room was divided by function, the north side yielding an old-fashioned wood stove, a careless array of books and magazines, a lounge chair. But the south side was all business, right down to the computer terminal and keyboard and file cabinets. The sophisticated equipment was very different from the easy mountain living style of the rest of the house, but surprised Trisha not at all. She knew that Kern kept an active interest in the complex corporation he had inherited from his father. She remembered all too well that his reputation in the business world had been ruthless. He had a perception and skill for maneuvering people and events that left competitors behind; nothing had ever stood in the way of what he wanted...

Her frown deepened as she studied the man she was so certain had not been in the house. A man alone—too much alone, she had seen that in him five years ago—and with a disquieting sense of déjà vu she suddenly saw the same man. Facing away from her, he was seated at the desk in the middle of the room, his fingers laced behind his neck and his head bowed. The room was so silent she could hear the ticking of the clock, but it was the silence in the man that troubled her, the look of tension and preoccupied weariness, the look of trouble...

She hesitated. "Kern?" she asked softly.

His head jerked toward her and she glimpsed
... what?—frustration? pain?—before he quickly masked
his features, his hands dropping and his shoulders automatically squaring back.

"I was doing some wash," she told him, explaining
her presence awkwardly, "and was just going to get a
cup of coffee. If you want one..."

"Thanks."

When she returned from the kitchen with a small tray,
he was standing, leaning back against the desk. The one
hand still worrying the tension at the back of his neck
dropped the minute he saw her.

"There's two aspirins on the tray for the headache,"
she said calmly.

"I don't have a headache."

"Of course you don't." She handed him a mug, which
he took, and then held out the aspirins in the open palm
of her hand.

He took them, glaring at her, a marvelously ferocious
scowl between bushy black brows that was thoroughly
wasted as he popped the aspirins and washed them down
with coffee. And then it was her turn to be irritated:
weariness erased itself from his eyes as he lazily surveyed
her figure from top to toe. The long slender legs, barefoot, the flapping yellow shirt at her thighs—he seemed
to know she wore nothing beneath. Perhaps it was written
on her breasts, she thought irritably, because that was
where he seemed to be staring, suddenly the image of a
perfectly relaxed man.

"You're deteriorating sadly, Tish," Kern said dryly.
"Every day you're here you seem to be going less and
less formal. From designer labels to jeans, and now to
a ten-year-old shirt and barefoot. By tomorrow I fully

expect you to be running around here stark—"

"I told you I was doing wash. I had no idea you were back in the house."

He cocked his head back, folding his arms across his chest. "I'll be damned if you don't manage to look like a princess even dressed like that, Tish. Every time I see that chin of yours go up and that haughty little nose of yours, I see the lady in her ivory tower. Inviolate, untouchable, pure. How is it you still project the same image?"

Once the mocking tone would have hurt, and badly; now Trisha just shook her head scoldingly at him, refusing to be drawn. "Do you want me to burst into tears because you're being so nasty or feel complimented at the princess image?"

"Damned if I know."

Her delicate eyebrows arched in teasing disbelief. "There must be monsoons if Mr. Lowery is suffering from indecision. At least a tornado. No?"

"God, you've gotten sassy," he commented with mixed exasperation and humor, motioning to the papers he had strewn on his desk. "You're also way off base, although there are times my mother does seem to have World War III potential in her. Or else for unknown reasons she's simply trying to drive me out of my mind."

Chuckling, Trisha perched on the arm of his lounge chair. "It can't be that bad."

"No? She used to be a damned good businesswoman, but a couple of years ago I asked her if she wanted me to handle her investments. It was around the time she started looking not very well to me, or at least not as well as I thought she should look. I was trying to lift the burdens a little, because she has quite an independent income from her mother's family, apart from the Lowery's..."

"And," Trisha prompted.

He threw up his hands in mock disgust. "There should be nothing to it, damn it. If I can keep control of a seven-figure business with quarterly visits and good management, it should be chicken feed to handle this bit on the side. Instead, my mother's been acting like she's on a leash for every con man this side of the Mississippi! I find myself a landlord of two rundown little apartment houses in Detroit, hassling sewer laws. There's some idiotic little bakery in Hamtramck she bought up for God knows what reason. She's set up some foundation for art-student scholarships—there's three-hundred little applications here to decide from. This one volunteered her portfolio ahead of time; as far as I know she's an expert at drawing squiggly lines..."

Trisha smiled, the proud tilt he'd accused her features of having now softening in empathy. Julia's cause took no deep thought to understand. "Perhaps it's her way of forcing you to make more and more trips up north, Kern."

His fingers laced behind his neck again as he stared at her. "All right," he admitted thoughtfully, "but it still doesn't make a hell of a lot of sense. We had a major war when I moved here, but that's long over with; she knows I'm settled here. And if she's lonely I've invited her here dozens of times. It's not as if we're close—though I've tried since my father died. God knows, the apron strings were cut when I was approximately five; mother's a long way from being a clinging personality..."

"You're right," Trisha agreed gently, "but she is growing older, Kern, and perhaps she's afraid of that. Alone, not quite well, and she doesn't . . . bend well. Maybe she doesn't know how to. She can't very well just come out and say she needs you, Kern."

Her voice trailed, the train of thought gone as she caught his expression intent upon her. His eyes were glinting something she never expected to see from Kern, the simplest sort of gentle warmth without even a hint of a sexual overtone. Had they ever shared a problem before? A warm glow kindled inside her, an awareness that she could almost believe in new beginnings . . .

"Kern?" said a vibrant voice from the doorway. "I knocked but when you didn't answer I just came in. I knew you'd have the work ready for me . . ."

Trisha stood up, nodding a polite hello to Rhea with shoulders promptly squared as though she were wearing her best evening gown. Kern had not mistaken her pride of bearing and it had to be in capital letters at the moment. Rhea had foregone mountain wear in favor of a stark white skirt and a matching jacket, a tasteful, not inexpensive outfit that did the most for a long stretch of darkly tanned legs. The long hair had been roped and coiled, and though the lady could not really claim classic beauty, there was an unmatchable pair of rich lustrous eyes fastened on Kern.

"And I should have known you'd come early for it," Kern said warmly, his hand extended in greeting to Rhea's. The hand was clasped, held.

"I'm sorry you couldn't make it to dinner the other night," Rhea ventured hesitantly to Trisha, her expression politely impassive as she noted the huge yellow shirt, half-dried hair, bare feet. "We had a wonderful time. Perhaps another occasion . . ."

Trisha smiled vaguely, snatching up the tray of dead

coffee cups as she ventured for the door. "You two are busy. I'll see you again at four, Kern, when we go to pick up your mother." It took an effort to close the door behind her with the awkward tray, but she managed it.

And then she closed her eyes for a full thirty seconds. Kern's warmth, his hand extended, the woman's sexual vibrations, their so-easily read ambiance . . . jealousy was a simple word. The sudden shakiness in Trisha's limbs was more than that, a despair in having to acknowledge how much she *did* care. Kern had accepted her back in his household easily, but she had no illusions as to his feelings for the long term. She was there because of his mother. She could be his bed partner if she wished it, but there was no question that he wasn't offering more. Why should he, after what had happened between them? One inhibited, skinny woman with a bad track record, next to Rhea, one of Rubens's treasures?

Hell, she murmured to herself as she clattered the cups in the dishwasher and tiptoed past the closed door to retrieve her wash. It was time to pull herself back together. Just the idea of Kern comparing the two of them was enough to make her shore up walls of pride against her crumbling confidence. Put competition in a sexual arena and all those tentative hopeful murmurings in the back of her mind were soundly buried.

At four Trisha was waiting for Kern in the driveway, the keys to the Mercedes restlessly swaying in her fingers. The mauve pantsuit shivered over her slim figure in the breeze, a subtle color that brought out the ivory in her complexion. Gone was the sunburned nose and windswept hair; in place was a mask of expert makeup and a sophisticated loose froth of curls, brushed back to show off a haughty profile. Trisha of Grosse Pointe was back and only the small pulse at the delicate V of her throat revealed any emotion at the sight of Kern's suited figure finally emerging from the house.

"You're late," she said curtly, as she opened the door to the driver's side and promptly slipped in.

More slowly Kern followed, eyes narrowed just slightly at her unexpected chill tone. By agreement they were taking the Mercedes over Kern's truck or jeep since they felt there would be more comfort and space for Julia. Yet there seemed no space at all once Kern folded in his long legs. In a dark suit Kern carried with him the brusque snapping sort of assurance she remembered from when she'd first met him, but these days the fabric seemed to strain at his shoulders as if the veneer of civilized man was only paper-thin. Hawklike features surveyed her new outfit, unfairly noting first the vulnerable V of her open throat before judging the aristocratic set of her profile. "You obviously had the urge to go shopping," he commented lazily. "If you needed money—"

"I managed," she said pleasantly, as she started the car and put her gold sandal intimately to the accelerator. She was about to become very good friends with speed. The chant in her mind all day had been to get Julia and get out before there was trouble—and as for the cost of the outfit, Julia would more than willingly subsidize the trip home, a thought that never seemed to have occurred before.

"Well, however you 'managed,'" Kern echoed deliberately, "the effect is cool and expensive, Tish. Lovely."

"Thank you." She saw his foot applying an imaginary brake as she rounded a curve too fast. Well, if he would just stop staring at her . . . "I had a terrific time shopping this afternoon," she said finally. "I saw a bundle of designs I could bring back home to my job; a few days of rest in the mountains and I feel invigorated all over again, full of plans and ideas."

"Anxious to go back to work, are you?" Almost too easily he was falling for the conversational gambit.

"Very much. This week I took a leave for Julia, but the three weeks after was vacation that I could probably reschedule for anytime."

"Had enough of mountain life in a few short days? It didn't take you long."

"Certainly not six months this time."

It hit home. The silence between them was abrupt, so tangible it could have been sliced. For a ridiculous instant Trisha felt the urge to cry, and then her rational mind soothed out as her driving did. She had cut her losses and run five years before, not as an act of cowardice but of self-preservation. This felt no different. The man beside her had disturbed, had already carved through old defenses she'd believed were invulnerable.

Half an hour later they were both seated in Ted Bassett's office. The doctor was standing with his hands dug the pockets of his white lab coat, unsmiling, his blue eyes darting back and forth between the two of them. "I wish I could tell you something definite," he said frankly. "Your mother just isn't a simple diagnosis, Kern. You already know about the heart murmur and that she had hypertensive blood pressure. People can have both conditions and live for years with proper medications. I can quote you the range of statistics if you want—"

"Forget that sort of thing," Kern said abruptly. "All I want to know is exactly where she stands."

"And that's just what I'm trying to tell you. Professionally, all I can suggest is that you insure she takes her pills, gets the proper rest, and maintains regular medical care. But . . ."

Trisha's frown of concern mirrored Kern's.

"But," Ted repeated gravely, "my gut instinct tells me she's stroke material. I'm not trying to alarm you. There's no real medical reason to justify that, but if you two know of anything at all that's worrying her . . ."

A short while later the two of them were out in the corridor. Trisha's sandaled heels clattered on the hospital tiles, her face as stark as the nurse's caps they passed. Kern, nearly a full head taller than she was, radiated a firm stride that halted abruptly several feet from Julia's closed door.

Trisha paused as well, glancing back at the sudden "don't-argue-with-me" slashed on his features. "I'm going to talk mother into staying here," he said flatly.

Her eyebrows raised as she shook her head. "Don't be silly, Kern. The only thing to do is take her home, around the things that she loves, the things she's familiar with—"

"You're the one who wants to go home, Tish. So you made a point of telling me earlier. But we both know what mother's worried about."

"What are you talking about?" Trisha asked him curtly, her eyes darting nervously at a passing patient who was plainly overhearing their conversation.

"The pair of us—that's what she's worried about. And since you're in such an all-fired hurry to get home, just go. Mother isn't leaving my sight."

Trisha drew in her breath at his unexpected bluntness. She felt slapped with guilt, knowing that what he said about the source of Julia's worry was true, and his cold "just go" put a sting to that slap. He really couldn't care less if she stayed or not . . ."I'm not leaving her here with you, Kern," she whispered furiously. "She hasn't cooked a can of beans in thirty years, and I don't see bridge clubs populating the mountains! What's she supposed to do with her time—watch you go out the door each day for ten hours? She happens to be the only mother I've got, too, and if only because I'm another woman, I'm the best one to take care of her."

"She's not leaving here."

"Would you just be reasonable—"

"I said, she's not leaving here, Trisha." He took three strides forward and raised an arm as if he were going to open Julia's door, as if the matter were already settled. Trisha grabbed at his sleeve to stop him, too angry and upset to even consider her words.

"Then I'm staying, too, Kern! At least until I see that she'll be happy. You can't possibly object when you know I could help her . . ."

He was looking at her slim fingers on his sleeve, and she dropped her hand quickly. The stone features were still prominent, but there was an odd half curl at the corner of his mouth, masked quickly when she stared up at him in sudden confusion. "For mother's sake, you'll stay for a while then," he said, dryly rephrasing her words.

Uncertainly, she frowned, her lips parted to say something—then nothing. Kern was already opening the door, greeting his mother in brisk, cheerful tones.

6

JULIA MAINTAINED A steady blaze of conversation from the moment they left her hospital room to the time they reached the Mercedes. With Kern on one side and Trisha on her other, captive listeners both, Julia was all too tempted to make the most of their mutual and obvious relief at seeing normal color in her cheeks again.

"...I never did have any tolerance for institutions. It's 'we'll' do this and 'we'll' do that and a wheelchair to move two feet across the hall. Half the time it's paper cups, and when they do come up with a glass it hasn't been washed properly. There's no butter for the bread, not a fried egg to be had. I told that little renegade of a nurse on the afternoon shift that I was old enough to determine cholesterol levels for myself, thank you very much, and as for privacy..."

Kern opened the front passenger-seat door for his mother, who then obstinately wanted to sit in the back. "You two sit together. I've grown quite accustomed to being completely by myself," Julia said petulantly.

"We'll have you home in no time," Kern said peaceably as he started the engine. "We were hoping you'd be hungry—"

"Of course I'm hungry. I haven't had a decent meal in two days. Trisha, I'm never forgiving you for talking me into that place. I am going *out* to dinner, Kern. I'm sure that child of a doctor told you that my blood pressure's back to normal."

Trisha leaned over the back of the seat. "But I've got lamb, darling," she said coaxingly. "With a mint sauce just like you love. The table's all set; it's just a matter of a quick reheating..."

"Wonderful. We'll have it tomorrow. I've been in this horrid wilderness for nearly four days and so far all I've seen of it is beds. It's no use your talking, Trisha. We are going *out*. And don't tell me Kern didn't know what was coming or he wouldn't have put on a suit."

"There was a debate between a suit or the spangled kind of T-shirt I don't seem to own," Kern said blandly. "I didn't really know if you would have to prove how healthy you are by insisting on a disco, Mother, or whether a simple restaurant would do—"

"Let's not be sarcastic." She added disparagingly, "Probably all you have in this place is a simple restaurant. I'm not difficult to please, Kern, although I do prefer a decent wine list..."

Kern parked on a side road off the main drag in Gatlinburg. Further down the road neon signs flashed a tourist's dream of motel choices, promising everything from waterbeds to video movies, in-room fireplaces, and live entertainment. Where the three of them walked were the shops, a clustered melange of attractive stores offering everything from imported Italian sandals to X-rated T-shirts. Christian Dior labels were back-to-back with a Native American crafts store, French antiques, Danish cheeses...

"Perhaps we'll go shopping tomorrow, Trisha," Julia

said thoughtfully, glancing suddenly at her daughter-in-law's pantsuit. "I haven't seen that before, have I? A marvelous color on you. So while I was stuck in the hospital you went shopping, did you?"

Trisha let go of Julia's arm long enough to divest her purse of a tiny wrapped package. "For you," she said mildly.

"To make up for forcing me into that place," Julia suggested, but her eyes softened on Trisha. "Well . . . thank you, Patricia. I'll open it when we get to the restaurant, if we ever do, Kern."

He stopped in front of a windowless brick-front building with a half dozen steps leading down to a glossy black door, unmarked and all but unnoticeable if it hadn't been for a single gas lantern shining on the steps.

"A basement, Kern?" Julia asked pleasantly. "I wish I could say I was surprised."

"Do you want to spank her or shall I?" Kern murmured to Trisha as a black-suited waiter led Julia first to a small corner table.

The impulse was to laugh. It took willpower to reject it, willpower not to share even an understanding smile with him when she knew they were both feeling equal quantities of exasperation and sheer joy at Julia's improved health. But it wouldn't do, Trisha knew, being drawn into that orb of male dominance, and she moved deliberately ahead of him, pretending not to see the way his eyes suddenly narrowed in catlike challenge.

Her attention was honestly captured by the restaurant in seconds. A manmade waterfall divided a small dance floor from the dining area, the sparkle of water through colored lights making rainbow prisms on the beamed ceiling. The pianist was playing semiclassical music, his touch gentle and relaxing. The wall as they'd come in was completely filled with wine racks. the bottles tilted, labeled so that anyone could choose their own. Candles and starched white linen, the sponge of soundless carpet and the heavy dark beams above, shadows and the irresistible pastel lights in the waterfall . . . it was all lovely.

Trisha was seated, suddenly conscious that Kern's fingers lingered on her shoulders as the waiter seated his mother. "I would have taken you somewhere else, but you did specify a wine list, mother," he drawled. "If you object to the 'basement,' though—"

"Sit down, sit down. Stop making a fuss," Julia said, scolding him, but the steel eyes were taking in the entire scene with the same undisguised pleasure that Trisha showed. With a sigh Julia settled back, allowing them all to relax while drinks were ordered. Her own wine she had chosen herself, a rosé from the Loire Valley. Trisha obediently ordered the drier pinot noir that Julia knew she would like. But Kern, predictably, listened to no one, insisting on his favorite whiskey straight up. "Well," Julia said finally as she sipped her rosé and looked at both of them, "are the two of you getting along?"

Trisha twirled the dark wine in her glass, watching the flame's reflection on the glass. "Of course we're getting along," she offered smoothly, not looking at Kern across the table from her. To expect Julia not to probe at the earliest opportunity would have been to expect rainbows served for breakfast. "And we've both been looking forward to showing you the area. I have all kinds of ideas for you . . ."

Throughout almost all of the dinner course, Trisha coaxed at Julia's interests, paying no attention to the dark-eyed man who persisted in disturbing her by staring from across the table. The Tennessee mountains were loaded with little out-of-the-way barn shops that sold antiques—one of Julia's loves. Clothes she liked as well, and Gatlinburg was not averse to stocking for expensive tastes. There was a professor at the camp who played bridge, as did Trisha; they only needed a fourth. And as far as the garden club Julia belonged to at home . . . "There's nothing to compare with what's here, darling, and June just couldn't be a better time. There are people who make annual pilgrimages here just to see the rhododendron in bloom. All over the heaths there's mountain laurel and Dutchman's-breeches . . ."

"One would almost gather you're taken with this place yourself, Patricia," Julia commented curiously.

Trisha heard the buildup of enthusiasm in her own voice, and became quieted. It was for Julia's sake, of course, and if there was a chance Julia would be happy here she would do her best to help, as she'd promised Kern. But he mustn't misunderstand. The waiter served coffee and after-dinner liqueurs. Trisha sipped at hers while the other two talked. The pianist inadvertently kept drawing her attention; from classical pieces he had switched to old, romantic love songs. Songs of lost love, forsaken love, loneliness, hope; melodies generations old in composing, timeless in theme . . .

"It's lovely, Patricia!"

Trisha drew her attention back to the tiny jade rose in Julia's palm, the present she had all but forgotten. "I thought you would like it," she said softly.

"It's just exquisite." Julia sighed with pleasure. "I'll have to forgive you both for the last two days, I suppose. Kern, I see the bandage is off your wrist, even if that scar still looks dreadful. What do you think, Trisha? You haven't told me whether or not you find Kern changed in five years."

No, Julia wasn't going to let it go, Trisha thought wearily. Her eyes met Kern's over the wineglass for the first time since dinner started. The candlelight played with his face, too, found hollows and valleys in the craggy features, reflected a soft texture to his beard and an untamed glint in his eyes. "He's changed a great deal," Trisha said lightly, her defenses bristling at that look. "We've become such good friends that he's even suggested I stay a little longer—that is, assuming you'd like to, Julia. Whatever you feel like doing will be fine by me." She suddenly had the ridiculous feeling that she should never have used the phrase "good friends." Ice barriers were a little different than thrown gauntlets, but then it was said, too late to take back.

"Well, I would like to stay for a least a few days, perhaps a week," Julia said vaguely with a faint frown. Trisha knew her answer was not quite what the older woman wanted. "And you, Kern," the older woman persisted determinedly. "You must be surprised at how much Patricia has changed . . ."

"Very," Kern agreed shortly. His features were still fixed on Trisha's, and with a sudden restiveness he stood up, offering his hand to her across the table. "You don't mind if we dance for a few minutes, Mother?"

Trisha shook her head. "I really don't think—"

"What a marvelous idea," Julia said cheerfully. "Take your time, both of you. I'll be perfectly content here with another cup of coffee. I like to rest for a while after dinner; you both know that."

His hand grasped hers, urging her up. Trisha felt all but herded to the far end of the room that contained the dance floor, the polite smile she had worn all evening for Kern now oddly fixed on her face. There were only two other couples on the floor. The pianist glanced up from his moody love song to smile lingeringly at her, but Kern whirled her around to face him. She sensed impatience and a sudden virulent voltage at his nearness that she ignored, as she had ignored it for hours, as she was going to continue to ignore it.

He hooked both of his hands at her waist, forcing her fingers to rest on his shoulders or be left awkwardly hanging in midair. She caught her breath when his fingers laced behind her, locking them breast-to-chest. "Kern, I think we should be taking your mother home. It might be too long an evening for her..."

"She's fine for fifteen minutes. The question is whether you can last that long, keeping that polite distance you've guarded all afternoon."

She drew in her breath. "I don't know what you're talking about."

His hand slipped up her back to the nape of her neck, and she found her arms around his waist. His fingers splayed in the soft disorder of hairstyle to force her face up to his. "You're more honest when you don't talk at all, Tish. So don't." It was an order and a warning; no smile touched his sensual mouth. His weathered cheekbones were taut and a sudden graven stillness came upon him. He stared down at her with eyes like liquid rock, and she felt his desire to possess.

She held herself stiffly when his hand forced her cheek to the soft silk of his shirt, her lashes low on her cheeks in an effort to hide the raw fear in the pit of her stomach. If he was trying to punish her for her coolness, or to prove for the sake of old revenge that she could no longer control her emotions around him—he was succeeding. The brush of a beard grazed her forehead; she found her arms encouraged tighter around his waist; and thighs grazing together in the motion of rhythm. The stroke of his fingers on the nape of her neck was deliberately soothing, gentling to her defenses. It was a painfully old love song the pianist kept playing, half love and half irretrievable loss, the melody suddenly aching inside of her.

Her body was finally molded pliant for him, just as he wanted. Almost despairingly she told herself that it didn't matter, that there was nothing that could happen on a dance floor. But it did matter—his lips pressed on her forehead and his arms tightened possessively around her as he felt her defenses falter. One hand slowly swept up and down her spine, molding her even closer. It was an embrace, not a dance; they both knew it. Yet she could not seem to move quite yet, with eyes closed absorbing the feel of his chest, his thighs in fluid movement against hers, his arousal alive between them...

And the pianist had his secrets, a way of cradling the words he sang with his tongue before he reluctantly set them free. There was no mike, only a throaty low voice not really trying to compete with the piano, just slowly measuring out a lingering poem of helpless longing...

> Should I stay?
> Would it be so wrong...
> If I can't help
> Falling in love with you...

The song she'd never heard before, but the rhythm seemed so old, so hypnotic, that she gave in finally. Like a drug she couldn't fight, her hips moved against his, feeling a sweet rush like champagne in her head. When she glanced up at his dark hooded eyes there was a sweet exultation in her own. Long ago she'd shied away from the fierce dominating passion she'd seen in Kern. His

eyes seemed like black fire, and the feminine in her felt
as potent as too much wine. Yearning ached through her
in almost a feverish rush; a need to increase the look of
desire in his eyes surged through her until there was no
going back. Her hands escaped slowly from his waist to
ripple gently over his chest, fingers climbing until they
found flesh, circled around to the nape of his neck and
threading in his hair. Her hips were cradled in his if she
moved just so, the rhythm like the music, a frictionlike
danger building between them as her swelling breasts
rubbed against his, as her thighs courted pressure . . .

She heard a harsh odd sound from the base of his
throat and looked up. There was almost a smile on his
lips. "Not here," he scolded chidingly.

"Only here, Kern," she corrected softly.

He shook his head. "You know better." He drew apart
from her. She was suddenly curiously aware that the song
was ended, and that it was not the same song they had
started out dancing to. Julia was looking their way, a
gentle smile on her mouth for the two of them. This *was*
a restaurant after all, other people . . . Then a disquieting
sense of déjà vu, of dancing with Kern and being be-
witched beyond all rhyme or reason came to mind.

Kern had a message from the camp when the three of
them got home, and for a short time he had to go out.
Trisha spent an hour settling Julia in and from there
wandered outside in the back. The grass was squeaky
with dew beneath her feet, and she slipped off her sandals, swinging them with one hand, feeling the damp
carpet curling around her bare toes. Stars peppered the
cloudless, breezeless night.

Her head ached just a little from the unaccustomed
wine. This time drinking in the clear mountain air, she

stood pensively for a long time. The mood from their evening was suddenly erased. The feeling of vulnerability seemed to be assaulting her from all sides—from the look of her face in the mirror when she was brushing her hair, from her every response around Kern, from each time she looked at the mist-swirling mountains and felt small and insignificant. Vulnerability was something she'd never wanted to feel again. It was an unwelcomed emotion.

Finally she heard the click of the door behind her. There was no reason to turn to know who it was. She'd been waiting for Kern. "I'm going to need some money," she said quietly.

"Fine."

She half turned then. His answer was almost humorously indifferent. Kern rarely smoked, and from where he was leaning against the house, the glow of ash sent up a whisper of smoke.

"Not for me," she said by way of qualification. "For your mother. I want to redo that room downstairs, Kern, in a style that would suit her. She thought it foolish at first, but I just reminded her that you had lots of space and you wanted her to have her own personal room when she came down for other visits. It might be a beginning, if she becomes attached to it." Trisha hesitated when he didn't comment. "She has expensive tastes, but I wouldn't overdo. I know what I'm doing with fabrics, Kern, and I know exactly what would appeal to her..."

"Don't be absurd, Tish. You know damn well there's money for whatever she wants—or you want," he said impatiently. "It bothered the hell out of me when I knew you were working and attending night school at the same time—"

"That was four years ago."

"And the checks I sent you all came back. Now are we done with that subject?" She could hear his heel crush the cigarette butt.

"Yes."

"And we suddenly have nothing else to talk about, do we, Tish?"

"Nothing." She shivered then, though there was no reason for it in the still warm night, and she moved forward to go inside. Barefoot when she came up the slope to Kern, to her he seemed taller than life, his head towering over hers. Her hand was on the doorknob when he reached out to stop her with an unexpectedly gentle hand. His fingers brushed back a strand of hair from her face and then his palm rested like a warm caress on her cheek.

"You're a giver, Tish. I'd expect you to come up with an idea for my mother. You've been there for her for years when you didn't need to be. She wasn't your responsibility. And you were there for me at one of the roughest times in my life—"

"Kern." Her fingers curled at his wrist, trying to dislodge the sensual palm.

"You haven't really changed. The look's very different, but you're still afraid to reach out and *take*, Tish, to take what's yours. I don't understand what you're afraid of. I never have," he admitted bluntly. "There's just . . . life. If you don't reach out and take what you want, there's nothing."

His fingers smoothed down her cheek, caressed her throat, and let go. She was still for a moment, feeling a sudden rush of confusion. Her image of herself had been the opposite of a "giver." She had failed to *give* him the response he needed in a wife. And what was he trying to tell her now? To seize this moment? Make love with him because the chemistry was there, as if there were no consequences? Was he even aware of how loud the words were that he *hadn't* said? There was no mention of her staying here beyond a short time. She had been the one who insisted on staying, for Julia. She hesitated, then said, "You find it easy to go after what you want, no holds barred, Kern. But I can't just—"

"You *can*. But if you don't, Tish, I will. I want you and I'll wait. But not long. Not anymore."

The clipped phrases seemed to emphasize the threat. Threat? It was a promise he was delivering in gentle tones that echoed in the night.

Trisha was doing her best not to punish the Mercedes on the deplorable little dirt road. Potholes polka-dotted every few feet of the narrow path, and dust sprayed behind them in thin sandy clouds. Oblivious to both the bouncing and the early morning heat, Julia beside her had a hand shading her eyes as she peered out the window. It was not the first time in the last four days that their goal was an antique shop, and Julia by the hour was thriving on every little adventure Trisha had thought up for her.

". . . what I want is one of those big iron kettles," Julia continued. "You know, the kind they used to hang in the fireplace. I thought I'd put it out on the front steps and plant it with flowers."

"We've seen a half dozen of them," Trisha remarked.

Julia smiled. "They were always asking too much. But today, I just have a feeling . . ."

Trisha grinned. Her mother-in-law was dressed in a loose shirt and trousers that were decidedly baggy. The raw silks had been put away. Julia did not want to be "taken" because she was a city slicker, but the overall new image invariably made Trisha chuckle.

The store they stopped at was more of a shed than any other sort of establishment. The cobwebs clung to the corners and Trisha wondered idly if the wizened old man actually thought there was some saving grace in four inches of dust and dirt. A cloud of it stirred as they stepped inside, their footprints distinctive on the wooden floor.

"You want something?" The old man rocked, watching their slow intrusion in his store.

"Probably not," Julia answered pleasantly.

Trisha fought the inclination to sneeze. There was barely room to navigate between the shaky wooden shelves packed into the shed, and each was filled with hopeful saleables, none of which had ever known a dust rag.

"Well, now..." He stood up, suddenly interested, sparing a glance for Trisha's lovely pink-jeaned frame and lighting on the deliberately worn-looking Julia. "You must have come out this way for something."

"Just looking." Julia fingered a cracked bowl disdainfully, set it up to view from a dusty window, and set it down again. Trisha marveled. It was a full ten minutes before the two even touched on the subject of iron kettles. Finally Julia nudged with her foot a cobwebbed kettle in the corner. "I suppose you're charging an arm and a leg for that."

"Well now..."

"Never mind. I can see the rust. All the work to clean it up—"

"From the first settlers that ever came to this area," the old man said firmly. "Earned its rust, it has."

"So *you* say. How much?"

"I thought twenty-five," the old man said cautiously.

"Oh, well." Julia turned to Trisha. "Remember the one we saw for twelve in Kentucky? I knew I should have gotten it then. Perhaps next month we could make a trip up..."

Julia had seen no kettle in Kentucky, Trisha knew well. Yet the fibs flew fast and furious. The huge wrought-iron kettle took on added age, makeshift tragedy in its past, a history involving wagon trains and Indian uprisings. Julia was incredulous at the price, the amount of work it would take to refurbish it, and simply could not believe it was quite what she wanted. It was over forty minutes before Trisha was able to get the kettle in the trunk of the Mercedes, and even then she had to wait while the two finished their bickering at the back door. Julia's smile was radiant as Trisha started the engine.

"Eighteen dollars!" She gloated. "An absolute steal! I haven't had such fun in ages!"

"I knew you liked antiques," Trisha commented, "but I always thought it was more the Queen Anne–type treasures—"

"Oh, no, my dear, it's the primitives I've always treasured. They simply don't belong in Grosse Pointe. Now, at Kern's it's a different story! Way back when I was first married I even liked to refinish the primitives; I like the feel of old wood and history around me."

"That from the lady who was ready to turn around after the first look at 'this wilderness country,'" Trisha murmured teasingly.

"Well, you're no better, Patricia! Five years of effort to teach you the difference between Shostakovich and Tchaikovsky, and you go disappearing into those woods every afternoon and come back looking like some... backwoods child!"

Trisha grinned mischievously. "Speaking of fashion, darling, when we get home I think I'll take a picture of you just as you look right now and send it back to Grosse Pointe. Backwoods child, is it?"

"Idle threat," Julia said peaceably, regarding Trisha's pink jeans and black-and-pink, scooped-neck sweater with suddenly narrowed eyes. "It's a good thing I took you shopping. I can't understand why Kern didn't do so to begin with. You could hardly have survived around the countryside in the few things you came with."

Trisha was silent, aware that she now had a closetful of purchases pressed on her by Julia. They would be repaid in time, when they were home, although Julia would argue about it. But taking things from Kern, even on a borrowed basis, had a very different cast...

"It really is very different here than I first thought," Julia admitted thoughtfully as they pulled up to Kern's house.

Trisha stepped out of the car to take out the kettle from the trunk. She understood too well what Julia was feeling, because the emotion was shared. The past days had been nothing like her life here before. She was continually more aware of how much she seemed to have missed five years before; and in trying to arouse Julia's interests she had been rather unwittingly arousing her own... a mistake, she knew. Once Julia was fully strong again, and in a position to make up her own mind if she could accept a move and be happy here, it was going to be difficult for Trisha to suddenly leave, and it didn't have to do only with Kern.

As Trisha stepped inside the cool hallway to the kitchen, she saw Kern sitting at the kitchen table with maps spread out before him. Julia bent to kiss her son on the forehead, smoothing down his hair as if he were a six-year-old with a cowlick, an image Kern presented not at all. "We've been having an absolutely wonderful time. Bought a tremendous old kettle. I'm going out in the woods after it cools off this afternoon and get some azaleas, I think, though first I'll have to deal with that rust . . ."

Trisha crouched down to take out from the refrigerator the tuna salad she had made earlier. In short order she had thin-sliced tomatoes to put on top and then added some slices of cheese, setting the tray under the broiler for a few short minutes. After pouring three glasses of lemonade, she reached on tiptoe for napkins from the top of the refrigerator—and turned to find Kern's slate-gray eyes all over her.

He could make her conscious as no other man ever had of exactly how her jeans fit, of whether or not her hair needed combing. She knew the sun had added color to her complexion, and there was even an added pound or two from a new appetite encouraged by so much exercise. In spite of herself she was becoming more and more relaxed until her eyes collided unexpectedly with that watchful, waiting look of his. Then she felt like snatching up the car keys and running. "What have you been up to this morning?" she asked calmly.

"It's what you two might like to be up to this afternoon that I was thinking about," Kern responded. "Around two I was hoping to talk you both into a helicopter ride."

Trisha frowned, taking the tray from the oven with a hot pad. "You know your mother isn't fond of flying, Kern."

Julia returned from freshening her hands in the bathroom. "An understatement, darling."

"Lately there've been more helicopters in the area than cars," Kern said absently. "The highest mountain ranges have been plagued with a tiny insect called a balsam wooly aphid. That bug is capable of destroying the entire adult Fraser fir population, and as yet there's no solution. Our one option is to spray out sterile aphids from a helicopter so that they'll mate with the damaging females. The 'girls' have only a short lifespan, so with no offspring their destructive habits are short-lived."

"I've never heard of such a thing," Julia commented. "I've heard of farmers spraying from planes..."

"Helicopters are more suited to the mountains," Kern explained, "because obviously they can go right down into the affected area."

"But you said it was a Smokies problem, Kern. Why do you have to get involved? Why don't the forest people just handle it? If you have to put your own time and money into something that's their problem—"

"Because the park is next to us, Julia, there are some problems that affect Kern's land too. It's not an issue of time or money," Trisha interrupted.

"Trisha, I wasn't attacking you," Julia chided primly. "For heaven's sake, it was just an idle comment! I swear you're getting as batty about this land as Kern is..."

Trisha drew in her breath, suddenly hearing herself as Julia seemed to. Kern had a fist propped under his chin, eyes glinting perfectly devilish amusement at her for taking on his cause. She stood up and cleared away the plates, turning away from him.

"Anyway, Kern, as far as going up in this helicopter, no. I never could handle air travel in any form. It was one of the reasons Trisha had to drive me here. But we haven't planned anything beyond a bridge game down at the camp late this afternoon, Trisha. There isn't any reason why you couldn't go with Kern."

"The outing was for you, darling," Trisha pointed out quickly. "I've lived here before. I know what the area looks like."

"I really don't want to play bridge anyway. Not today. I want to fool with my kettle."

"Then I'll help you . . ."

There was a little silence, in which she could almost hear the echo of her own voice protesting too much. She did not want to go anywhere with Kern. She knew it and he knew it, but to this point she had the excuse of keeping a careful and continual eye on Julia's health. The lady whose darting eyes surveyed both of them now denied that need, a fresh bloom of color in her cheeks, the shine of rest and renewed health in her eyes . . . Trisha turned from them both and heard Kern's chair scrape back as he rose.

She bent to set the tray in the dishwasher, and when she stood back up Kern was there. His wrists rested loosely on her shoulders, pinning her at arm's length. His shoulders were wide enough to effectively block out Julia, kitchen, everything but Kern in front of her. One finger reached up to lazily smooth the hair from her cheek. "Trisha just wants to make sure you're happy, mother. That's all Tish is interested in. You'll have to convince her you wouldn't feel deserted if she left you for a couple of hours."

The teasing tone was boyish; the look in his eyes was strictly a man's. There was seduction in his eyes, and when she stooped down below his arms to escape from him, there was Julia again. Keeping the lady happy was how she justified being here.

"I would *not* feel deserted for a couple of hours." Julia almost snorted. "You'd think I was some sort of invalid!"

Trisha sighed and gave her mother-in-law a smile. "Well, then—of course I'll go," she managed to say finally, before turning back to Kern in defeat.

Matthew Redding landed on an open stretch of land near Kern's camp. A thin, well-weathered man in his forties, he wore coveralls and a smile that didn't know how to quit. "Mr. Lowery, you didn't mention we were taking a passenger!"

So much for Kern's plans for ever taking Julia. "I'm Trisha, Matt," she said, extending her hand. "Let's keep it on informal terms."

"And we sure will do that, honey. We're going to be on close terms real quick. The old bird's set up for two—three in a pinch. And a pinch is what I call first-name terms!"

Laughing, Trisha vaulted up into the bubblelike cubicle, eyeing the control panel with an amateur's enthusiastic interest. Kern folded in on her right as Matt settled in at the controls, the pilot turning to her with an impish grin. "You really don't mind it cozy?"

"No problem. I love these things!"

"No nerves about flying in one of them?"

"No." Trisha shook her head exuberantly. "I've clocked in a few hours in a little single-engine Cessna, but never a copter. I'm really curious to know the difference."

"You *what?*"

It was a delight to shock those all-knowing gray eyes for once. Kern's arm stretched across the back of the seat to make more room for all of them, also making it all but impossible for her to settle anywhere comfortably but in the curve of his shoulder. Which she did, facing Matt. Her annoyance at being roped into the venture had all but disappeared. "It was nothing, really. Instead of a vacation last year, I spent the money on a few flying lessons. Didn't get enough for a pilot's license by any means, just got a taste—or should I say a tease? I've always wanted to fly," she admitted wistfully.

"Good," Kern murmured next to her ear. "You can finish your lessons here and take over the copter. Then I can send this old reprobate back to Detroit where he belongs."

"This is yours?"

Kern nodded, motioning impatiently to his wrist, as if to say that the temporary impairment had forced him into hiring the pilot in the interim. The noise of the whirling propellers promptly deafened all other sounds. They were off the ground in a moment, heading directly over the treetops. Matthew handled the controls as if the bird were a well-loved toy that thrived on being played with, his turns sharply angled and his ups and downs deliberate. Trisha found herself laughing at the sudden roller-coaster sensations in her stomach, and Matt's grin was sheer showing off.

But it was not a sightseeing trip they were on, regardless of what Kern had said, and it didn't take long for Trisha to realize it. It was a swift pace to one spot, a hover, and then a repeat of the same. The men attempted no verbal communication over the rhythmical whirr of the helicopter blades.

Once they were off Kern's land, Trisha lost track of landmarks, and distances were deceivingly different by air than by road. The day was cloudy, the sun occasionally casting a lemony haze on stretches of forest as they passed. From the miles of lush green forest there was suddenly a narrow patch of barrenness illuminated by sunlight, where a few stalky pine trunks were bleakly standing. There the earth was grayish rather than the rich

brown that would have been natural. Ash. Trisha felt a
lurch of horror at the fire's devastation, but already they
were moving on.

More of the lush fairy-tale green appeared, and the
crystal of a stream one could see winding for miles. The
splash of a waterfall was half hidden in trees, and just
beyond was a heath, thick with flowers—purple-white,
then the flame of azalea; perhaps a hundred acres of
rhododendron alone. And then the barrenness again—a
long ragged oblong patch this time. The fire had been a
season ago, she was told, and now green was trying to
make its way through the odd-colored soil in erratic patterns of new life.

"You want to see what happened ten days ago?" Matt
shouted to Kern. "It's down to your right."

Unconsciously she pressed closer to Kern to see. She
felt his hand smoothing back her hair and raised stricken
eyes to his. This had been their land, once. Kern's eyes
met hers, inducing an unconscious tremor that pulsed
through her body. His hand stopped its stroking and his
fingers rested at the nape of her neck as they both looked
out where Matt was hovering.

The bleak scene below was not large, a tribute to how
rapidly the forest rangers reacted to a fire. Thousands of
acres that might have been affected were not. Still, all
Trisha could think of was a match being set on Kern's
land and what the land meant to him.

Matt headed back. "Fraser firs sure lookin' better on
your side of the ridge than on the Smokies side," he
called over her to Kern.

"Too soon to tell. The agriculture people will be here
next week. We'll see what they say," Kern answered.

"There hasn't been a fire for over a week."

"Yes, but it's too damned dry."

"When are you going to take your turn at the controls, Trisha?" Matt turned to her with a teasing grin.

"As long as you've got crash helmets to put on..."

When they landed, Trisha wandered off to the jeep to wait while the men talked for a few more minutes. The whirring sound of the propellers was still in her ears, and she felt a strange mixture of exhilaration and disquiet from the ride. It was not easy to forget what she'd seen.

Kern finally strode from behind her, patting her fanny as if to tell her to get a move on and get in. She moved so quickly to get into the jeep that he laughed at her. "Well, bright eyes. Bringing up secrets from the deep, are we? Looking for a pilot's job in the mountains?"

"Certainly," she quipped back as he started the engine. "Barring a minor matter of a license and experience, of course."

"Of course. Once upon a time I piloted a single-engine Cessna myself, but the license doesn't extend to copters, and it seems I just haven't found the time to go after it. But—fires, this aphid thing in the Fraser firs, marauding bears and wild boars, a missing camper on occasion— it occurred to me last winter that a copter's a fast way of keeping control—"

"And a most intriguing little toy," Trisha suggested innocently. "As Julia would say, the only difference between a man and a boy is the price of their toys."

"Now don't get sassy." His eyes flickered over her, a grin slashed above the ebony beard. "If you're nice to me, I might just sign you up for lessons."

"Talk, talk, talk." The wind was whirling her hair so helter-skelter in the open jeep that she put both hands up impatiently, capturing a tousled knot at the top of her head.

He braked the jeep and they both climbed out. "Hold

it." Kern leaned folded arms over the side of the vehicle, an expression on his face that she couldn't quite fathom, but the teasing look was gone. "Were you just talking about wanting to fly?"

Trisha let her hair fall in a tumble to her shoulders, reaching in for her purse on the floor of the jeep. "No. I've always wanted to fly," she admitted. "But it's just a dream, Kern, the way opening a crafts shop for me was once a dream I had here."

"You never told me you wanted to do that."

She shrugged, tossing back her hair, aiming for the house. "There's irony somewhere. The dream was the selling of authentic Cherokee designs and the back-country quilting patterns; the reality's been in dealing with plain old polyester on a mannequin." She turned to smile at Kern as she opened the door to the house. "The ride was fun. Thank you very much."

She waited. Kern hadn't accepted being dismissed with civilized politeness before. He had always taken advantage of the few moments they had had alone. And the hall was empty, dark, and quiet. But he just stood there, waiting for her to go inside, his eyes resting on hers with the awareness of a hawk's. Suddenly embarrassed, Trisha hurried past him. He's got you waiting for him to seduce you, she thought irritably. Less forgivable to her was knowing that she'd been standing there, not only anticipating but counting on it.

7

"LORD, NO! I just got my feet up after traipsing around all day. If you two would just leave, I could kindly treat myself to a forbidden glass of Cognac, close out all the disgusting fresh air in this house, and write some letters." Julia repeated it just in case either Kern or Trisha had missed the point. "I do *not* want to go on some little mystery excursion anywhere at eight o'clock at night."

Trisha sighed, staring glumly at a fixed point between Julia and the waiting Kern. The impulse, really, was to curl up in a chair and simply fall asleep. After a long day of shopping to decorate Julia's room, she had been too tired to more than peck at dinner, and she hadn't taken off the outfit she'd worn all day: a slim olive skirt slit attractively to show off her legs, an ivory silk blouse with a crisp V neck and long sleeves. It was attractive on her but swelterlingly hot. Hot, tired, and vaguely restless, she was in one of those moods where she really didn't know what she wanted.

A few minutes later she was out in the darkness with

Kern, not at all certain why she had agreed to come. He'd simply spoken of an hour's outing and something he thought she'd be interested in, not worth worrying about if she wasn't. His indifference had doubled her sense of restlessness inside. For two days now the black-shirted, charcoal-jeaned man at her side had radiated such quiet that Trisha was beginning to feel like the stranger she was supposed to be in his house.

Lord, you're mixed up, she told herself with silent disgust as they drove through the night. Tree shadows were impossibly still on the road, not a stirring of life. Mountain nights promised to be cool, but this one was tepid, clinging, the breezes too tired and hot to try. The full moon was gone and the next seemed too lazy to come out.

He stopped the car in less than twenty minutes. Instinct told Trisha that as the crow flew, they couldn't be more than a hop and a skip from his own home. The log cabin in front of them radiated warmth from within, an old rambling structure with the scent of horses wafting from a nearby building. A yard light beaconed on the gravel drive of the rustic mountain home.

Trisha stepped from the car, knowing instinctively she should have changed into jeans. Rarely accustomed to being moody for long, she could not seem to shake the feeling that tonight she just wasn't going to do anything right.

Kern threw an arm on her shoulder as they approached the three-stepped porch. She debated shrugging off the arm or cuddling closer. By the time the door opened, she was still mulling over decisions she just wasn't in the mood to make that day.

Rhea stood in the doorway with the lamplight behind her. "Well! Why didn't you say you were coming?" She

scolded Kern. "Hello, Trisha." A free and easy welcome
to Kern, a guarded one to Trisha; any sensitive ear would
have heard it. The lady wore skin-tight white jeans and
a loose black T-shirt that scooped seductively over voluptuous breasts. "Come in!"

"I want you to show Tish what's in your back room,
Rhea. I knew you wouldn't mind."

"Of course not, just glad for the visit. Make yourselves
comfortable while I get us something to drink."

The main room of the cabin was outfitted with overstuffed chairs, all designed to curl up in. A piece of
needlework had been set aside in one of them, a pattern
Trisha frankly coveted. Warm lights brightened the fur
rug on the floor and the handmade crewelwork on the
wall. Rhea brought tall drinks of gin and tonic, and Trisha
gratefully accepted one. Make herself comfortable in
Rhea's home? She'd never credited Kern with sadism
before.

For a half hour the devil leaned back in one of those
comfortable chairs, an ankle resting on his other leg's
knee, swirling the drink in his hand, looking both lazy
and completely comfortable. Perched a distance from
both of them on the edge of an old-fashioned love seat,
Trisha finished two glasses of the liquid rapidly. She was
feeling distinctly unnerved and smiling like mad as the
other two had an easy conversation. Rhea stood with her
back to the rough-hewn walls and her long braided hair
swayed as she moved. The black lustrous eyes rarely left
Kern's although there was no question that she was polite, even overtly friendly to Trisha.

When the first pitcher of drinks was done, Rhea strode
back into the kitchen to make another.

"Come closer," Kern suggested when Rhea was out
of sight. "You're hiding over there in that corner like a

kitten just brought home." He patted the arm of his chair, but there was a wealth of awareness in his eyes for the awkwardness she knew she was showing. "You'll like her if you give her half a chance, Tish."

"I like her now," Trisha responded politely. "Are we going home soon?"

Kern burst into laughter as Rhea came back in. Trisha stood up to accept her third drink, already regretting that she hadn't had dinner but not willing to stop. But it was hot. There was a thirst inside her that simply wouldn't be sated.

"Come with me," Rhea invited. "I'll show you my special back room."

It was certainly a better choice than behaving like an idiot in front of Kern. The first two gin and tonics were working and the third she clung to like a security blanket, following the tall woman down a long, narrow hall.

"When my husband died, I got into this," Rhea said quietly. "For six months I barely left this room. Kern mentioned yesterday that you used to be interested in this sort of thing . . ."

The "little something he thought she'd be interested in" was a quilting frame, and momentarily Trisha rallied. The frame took up most of the room, and she had an immediate picture of history, of mountain women seated around the diamond-star pattern, buzzing of their lives and loves a hundred years before. A long low trunk stood in one corner, and Rhea opened it, taking out a dozen finished quilts. Some had well-known designs and others were obviously Rhea's own.

"I'm sorry about your husband," Trisha offered quietly. She heard what wasn't said, that six months of shutting herself away with painstaking work must have been the only way Rhea knew to deal with her grief.

Compassion touched Trisha for the other woman. It had nothing to do with Kern. "I've never seen some of these patterns except in books. I've got one I made at home, Rhea, but I could never match your skill with a needle."

"I thought at first about selling them, but somehow at the time I just put them away and sort of forgot about them."

Trisha fingered the lovely work. "I don't know how you could sell them. They're more like heirlooms."

Rhea half smiled. "Not these. These I'd like to get off my hands, to tell you the truth. They remind me of a very bad time. Kern told me yesterday that you had something to do with marketing clothes. If you have any ideas . . ."

The confession she'd made to Kern flashed back to Trisha, of the shop of mountain crafts she'd once wanted to have. It was a passing comment at that moment, but he had heard. As a buyer she had a flair for marketing, far more than direct skill with a needle herself. And the old dream? In her mind she could already see a shop and feel the joy of being her own boss. Rhea would know others who wanted their crafts sold . . . Trisha looked up, about to say something to Rhea, and then stopped herself, finishing her drink instead. How many times did she have to remind herself that her time in the mountains was short-lived? It must be the alcohol that made her want to suggest something to Rhea as if they could be friends.

They lingered for a time in the room, talking the neutral subject of crafts. Words flowed with surprising easiness, though surely they were both equally aware of a second layer of tension in the room. Finally Rhea stood up to leave.

"Kern was good to me when my husband died," she mentioned a little awkwardly. "I was holed up here for one whole winter and might have been here still if he hadn't pushed me back into the outside world. People think a lot of him in this area."

"I know," Trisha said quietly.

Still Rhea hesitated in the doorway. "I didn't know he was married before. And I don't know why the two of you were separated. Nor do I want to; it's none of my business. But I would like to ask you..." Rhea hesitated. "I would like to ask you if you're staying here or going north." Those liquid dark eyes bored into hers, clear and still. "I've always spoken plain English," she said quietly. "I won't lie to you. Kern's never offered me anything but friendship, and I would never come between husband and wife. But if you are returning..."

That the woman was being fair nagged at Trisha like a headache. Her earlier impressions of Rhea were already dropping like hot cakes. It was a great deal easier to rack up dislike for a sultry femme fatale. Instead Rhea was simply a very quiet woman, radiating integrity, requesting an honest answer to an honest question that Trisha didn't know how to give her. Yes, she was going north again. No, she didn't want Rhea anywhere near her husband. "Perhaps we could talk another time," Trisha said awkwardly, miserably remembering the morning she'd all but thrown Rhea out of Kern's kitchen.

For a few more minutes they congregated in Rhea's kitchen, a cozy little room made more so by the three bodies trying to move in it. Rhea fixed some sort of snack that she and Kern devoured and Trisha pretended to. Food just wasn't going to get past the lump in her throat, but the alcohol kept trying to, and one of them seemed to have stuck yet another drink in her hand.

"I almost forgot, Kern," Rhea said. "You mentioned

you'd look at Satin for me the next time you were over. The vet was just here, but the closer she comes to foaling . . ."

"Of course."

"I know it's late," Rhea said apologetically to Trisha.

"I don't mind," Trisha assured her. "I'll just stay and wait on the back porch." She followed them out, smoothing her skirt behind her as she perched on the top step, leaning wearily against the porch railing. The porch was weaving beneath her after the last drink she'd had, but the sky above was salted with clear-cut stars. The other two walked off into the yard, two distinct black heads, silhouetted as a pair by the yard light.

It struck her later that she only saw one. The one she loved. The shape of his head and the way he walked, the way his jeans fit, his hands. She watched until he disappeared into the building. Then something akin to fear braced through her system when she could no longer see him. The idea of no longer being able to see him when she left and how she had wasted the time five years ago, too blind to see who he was and what he was offering her so freely then, swept into her mind. She closed her eyes, troubled, weary, unforgivably dizzy.

The two of them strode back from the horse barn just a short time later. Kern had his hand on Rhea's shoulder, offering her a good-bye as they neared the porch. Trisha stood up so quickly her head reeled. It seemed there were two Rheas she politely thanked before gratefully heading for the car. Something caught on her sandaled toe and she tripped, righting herself promptly, a stain of embarrassed color shadowing her cheeks. "Clumsy," she murmured to Kern.

"Is that the problem," he responded dryly. A not ungentle hand folded around her slim shoulders, curling her easily in the hollow of his body. Her hand slipped around his waist, the clean male scent of him suddenly far more intoxicating to her senses than anything she had had to drink. He opened the car door, encouraging her inside.

"Wait a minute, I . . ." She touched her head dizzily. "I think I forgot my purse."

"It's next to you." He was chuckling at her as he closed the door. He opened his own and slid in, surveying her from head to toe with another chuckle. "Lord, are you tipsy, Tish!"

"I've never in my life had too much drink," she informed him with dignity, and promptly leaned her head back against the seat so the car would stop spinning. Gold strands of hair fanned the seat back. Her skirt seemed to have slipped up to her thigh. Her shoes had slipped to the car floor. Humiliation was intense for being such a total fool as to over drink—no less for everything she seemed to have done or said the entire evening—but glancing down at herself there just seemed so very many little things to try to correct . . .

He leaned over before starting the engine, brushing her soft lips with his own, so gently, so sweetly that she melted against him, eyes closed, her fingertips just barely caressing his neck. "And aren't you human," he murmured against her. "The civilized veneer keeps disappearing, Tish . . ." He pulled back, starting the engine, and then as if on second thought pulled her deliberately closer to him, her head encouraged to lean against his shoulder and her feet tucked under her on the seat.

There were no lights and no sign of other cars on the black road home. Just the two of them on a quiet night, a warm sensuous mist drawing down into the valleys, drifting in the rich perfume of wildflowers and forest freshness. The shelter of darkness soothed the grating unhappiness inside her; she was where she wanted to be, next to him, touching, alone. She was too weary and too light-headed to raise any defenses.

The car stopped in front of his house. The lights were off from within; Julia had gone to bed hours before. Kern opened the car door and held out his hands. She took them, uncurling from the car seat to reach immediately for him, her cheek to his chest and her arms folded around his waist before the dizziness could upset all of her equilibrium again. "Kern . . . I want you to make love with me."

He drew in his breath, his hands tenderly smoothing back the hair from her face, smoke-colored eyes searching her features. "You were jealous, Tish," he murmured. "Do you think I don't know that? Come on now, it's late . . ."

"I am jealous," she agreed just as softly. "That isn't why, Kern. And it isn't the alcohol, although maybe that makes it easier to say it. What you do with Rhea in the future, or what we did in the past . . . I'm only talking now, Kern. I'm not asking for more and it's not easy to say . . ."

He kissed her, softly and lingeringly, the beard brushing against her cheek in sensual roughness. She curled her arms around his neck, wanting him closer, craving him closer. His lips were still molded to hers when she felt the sweep of his arms beneath her thighs, the solid ground lifted from beneath her.

He kissed her again, striding into the house. The side of her head was cradled to Kern's shoulder. She could hear and feel his thumping heartbeat as if it were part of her. He *was* part of her.

Rhea was perhaps the better mate for Kern. Trisha was not fighting that, or the past. The only thing that seemed to matter was that she take the only chance she might have, that the moment not be allowed to slip through her fingers like shifting sand. She had love to give him at this moment, a love that ached for the scar on his forehead and his laughter, for the land he cherished and even the problems it brought him. And for the feel of his body covering hers. It was a moment she had to take and she knew that it was right; inside was such a vibrant surge of need that she could not deny it...

He laid her gently on the bed, sitting next to her, not turning on the light. The room was warm and dark. The covers that he'd dragged down first left silk-cool sheets, her hair tousled against them. Shadows in the room showed a face grave above her, strangely silent, watching.

His hands moved. With frustrating slowness he unbuttoned her blouse, resisting her hands when she tried to help him. So she lay still, her eyes never leaving his. The blouse was slipped from her shoulders and dropped. The skirt had a side button and zipper; he found them, shivering the skirt down over her hips and releasing it to the floor as well.

Coolness feathered over her skin, a coolness she had not felt through the long sultry day and evening of too many clothes. His eyes warmed that odd little chill, shining black in the night-darkened room. Her body was silvery light by contrast, slim supple limbs, the sensual hill and valley of woman, her eyes open to his. She was vulnerable—not caring; and pleading—not caring.

He raised her up to undo the bra. Her body was faintly

trembling, a dew of moisture like satin coating her flesh. Her blood was on fire, waiting. The briefs covered so little, yet they were the most difficult to take off. His palms chased them slowly down her thighs and calves, intimate, erotic. She was burning. The aching inside seared; the effort to lay still was monumental.

"You're the most beautiful woman I've ever known, Tish," he murmured huskily. "I want you like something—clawing inside of me. I always have. Your skin is so soft..."

He was silent, but when she reached up with trembling hands he simply clasped them, held them in an iron-fast hold, and then let her go. The sheet was smoothed to her breasts; he leaned over to press a tantalizingly sweet kiss on her forehead. A brother's kiss. Shocked sapphire eyes watched him stand erect. "No, Tish, not tonight," he murmured. "I don't want Dutch courage between us. It matters too much—not for me, but for you."

He was gone, and the war began inside her. She had the urge to slip into his room, insisting as if she had no pride...the urge to sleep off the wretched dizziness...the urge to weep with frustration and confusion. And last, just as the dawn glowed a rainbow haze in the mountain valley, came the urge to laugh. They had changed roles and she saw the irony. How well he had paid her back for the night by the stream and the night they had been dancing. The tease he had invoked when undressing her she knew had been deliberate torture...

The thought ached inside that somehow it was going to be nearly impossible to leave him if they made love, but a second thought overshadowed the first as sleep finally overcame her. She could not leave him again with that old impression of five years ago, of a woman cold, too inhibited and too frightened to take what there was in life.

Trisha backed up to the doorway, brushing a sheen of moisture from her forehead before resting her hands on her hips. No one would have recognized Julia's room from the way it looked two weeks ago. The heavy oak furniture had been replaced by wild cherry of a more feminine mode, and the soft blue of the carpet and spread and draperies richened the effect of the wood. Julia's love of flowers had spilled over onto the vases on each side of the bed, and the bedside tables had been a find: old, intricately carved tobacco stands from another century, the copper inside glowing like new pennies. An old mirror had been another find: resilvered it reflected all the clutter on the dresser that made it a woman's room—perfumes and the cloisonné brush and comb Julia always carried with her.

"A perfect little hideaway," Julia said from behind her. With a radiant smile she surveyed the room with both approval and pleasure. "But there was no need for you to work yourself to the bone, Patricia, particularly today! The curtains would have waited. It must have been a hundred and ten on that ladder! Now stop altogether. I've got lunch all set up outside today."

"Done! Just give me two minutes to freshen up," Trisha told her. Walking to the bathroom, she could hardly wait to splash cool water on her hands and face. She was more than pleased with the work she'd done, and her easy smile showed in the reflection in the mirror, as did a little rueful arch of her eyebrows as she glanced at herself. There was a bit of a stranger in the mirror. The emerald and navy halter top and matching shorts were an outfit she'd insisted to Julia she'd never wear, but the heat had convinced her that morning to change her mind. Still, she was not accustomed to dressing with so much skin showing, and her hair was beginning to look as if she'd professionally streaked it, a natural silver added to the gold just from being in the sun. Her skin had a light honey cast.

"Patricia, are you still working?" Julia called out.

With one last flick of the brush, Trisha set it down and hurried out to the patio. "You really do have it all set up out here," she commented, sinking promptly into a lounge chair with feet up in the heat. The picnic looked delectable, or would have if she'd been less broiling, simply less overweary from a night of too little sleep.

"I'm going fishing this afternoon."

Trisha blinked. "I beg your pardon. I could have sworn you just said . . ."

"I expect I shall hate it." Julia poured three glasses of iced tea, molding a napkin around Trisha's to absorb the moisture before handing it to her. "Don't ask me why I'm going, the very idea of fishing . . . well, Mr. Michaels has a degree in agricultural economics, and he was so very nice about it, and I might as well do something one does in this sort of country . . ." Julia sat ramrod straight in a lounge chair, weaving her hand like a fan in front of her face.

"I don't think you should be going out for an entire afternoon in this heat without a rest," Trisha commented.

"Oh, don't you?" Julia said dryly. She leaned forward, adjusting a wrought-iron footstool with a bright yellow cushion for her feet. "You persist in trying to manage me! Speaking of which, how long are we staying here, darling?"

The casual question was enough to make Trisha lean

her head back and regard her mother-in-law with narrowed eyes. "Well, that depends on how happy you are here, of course," she said lightly.

"I'm all very nicely settled in here, as you very well know. In fact, I decided the second day we were here that I'm going to spend some of the time with Kern and some of the time up north. We'll split up the year or something. When he's had enough of me, I'll just go back to Grosse Pointe—hopefully in time for the start of the symphony season. I haven't mentioned it, because I've been waiting for Kern to have the nerve to tell me that I need a medical watchdog full time."

Trisha couldn't control an impish smile, seeing the wheels turn in Julia's mind at the anticipated argument. It was settled, but Julia would bring some drama into it.

"However, I wasn't referring to myself, Patricia, but to you. Surely the two of you have talked by now. Anyone with eyes in her head can see that the only time Kern has his eyes off of you is when he's sleeping. But you, darling, are not such an easy read. Now have you or haven't you two decided to try and make a go of it?"

When Julia's tone was the most innocent, her eyes were the most steellike. Trisha turned away, sipping at her iced tea and then setting it down. It suddenly occurred to her that Julia was dotting all the i's in rather earthquake fashion: her future was settled; her room was done; her health and humor were back on an even keel. All the reasons Trisha had stayed for. To stay beyond that required an invitation that had not been forthcoming.

"I see," Julia murmured into the little silence. "You're expecting him to say it all, when you happened to be the one who walked out on him five years ago."

"Nothing is simple," Trisha said quietly, stung by the accusation delivered so mildly. "Leave it, please."

"Either you love him or you don't."

Trisha vaulted up from the lounge chair, flicking back her hair with a brisk toss, and leaned over to kiss her mother-in-law's forehead. "Darling, you're so damned healthy again that I'm inclined to tell you to mind your own business. But I won't, of course, I love you too much, no matter how meddling you are. And you're getting freckles on your nose, Julia. *Most* unacceptable in a lady of sixty-seven."

Julia's hand promptly darted to her nose as if one could wipe away the offending subject. In those few seconds Trisha was already putting distance between them. "Wait a minute, Patricia! Where are you going? There's lunch—"

"I'm not hungry," Trisha responded over her shoulder. "And once you have lunch, you take a half hour rest before going out, Julia. Do you hear me?"

It had been a long time since she'd tried to find the place. There was a woody ferned area that was almost impenetrable, but only for a short distance. And then it was a craggy climb where the trees grew at crazy angles to reach the sun on the sharp slope. She could hear the sound of water falling halfway up the climb, and already the rest of the world had disappeared—no houses, no roads, no human sounds intruded. It was so high up that there were faint wisps of misty clouds on a level with her, guarding the secret of a place, a secret she'd kept within herself for more than five years.

And then there it was. Tired, hot prickly . . . Trisha stood still and surveyed her haven. The water fell from the cleavage of two smooth-breasted rocks fifteen feet above, splashed down to an almost perfect circular pool, and escaped in a little trickling stream down the mountain, beyond her sight. Surrounding the pool was a mix of huge, sun-warmed boulders and stretches of velvet moss, where a profusion of flowering bushes nurtured patches of shade. The pool itself was bedded with rocks so white they resembled snow flecked with gold in the sunlight. The taste of the water was almost sweet, bracingly cold; and it had the look of jewels of a treasure: the sunlight put diamonds in the waterfall, opals in the clear reflecting pool, and purest gold in the pool bed, emeralds in the brush nearby.

As far as she knew, no one knew of the place, not even Kern. Long ago she had had no excuse for going so far off the trail, no possible reason to make a path when it was clear no one had traveled there before. The peace had been there like a promise five years ago, and she craved it now. She perched on a flat oblong rock with her knees tucked up and her eyes closed, willing the sun to melt away the chill of heartache Julia had invoked.

An invitation from Kern for a renewal of commitment—no, there hadn't been one. Julia's busy eyes had interpreted physical desire as something else in Kern, but Trisha had never expected more. She was the one who had failed him in the past and she could not blame him for not offering second chances. And for just this moment she was not even going to let herself believe how painfully she wanted that second chance. There would be time for that when she was home again, time for despair and a twisting, sharp sort of anguish that even now was trying to shred and tear inside. She opened her eyes.

Not now. Not this moment. This moment is just . . . free, she told herself. She stayed absolutely still until the peace of the haven penetrated, past mind and heart and skin, as if the sun could heal soul—and like a gift, the peace was there.

The rock was hot, and restlessly she uncurled to stand, her canvas-shoed foot slipping into the chilling stream as she did so. It was delightfully cold. In a moment she had both shoes off and then with increasing speed all the rest of her clothes. The pool was only three feet at its deepest, ideal for cooling off if not swimming. She stepped precariously from rock to rock with her arms raised for balance, the sun hot and vibrant on her flesh, the icy water lapping at her knees. The waterfall drew her irresistibly.

There was no one around to hear her startled laughter as the weight of icy water streamed through her hair and over her slim body in torrents. She stood as long as she could stand it, until finally, with her skin tingling fresh and pink, she breathlessly struggled back again over the slippery round rocks of the pool to the flat rock at the edge. The heat of the smooth stone felt good and she perched with her toes stretched to the water, raising her face to the sun.

The sun dried and pearled a luster to her skin in minutes. The lush primitive landscape seemed to reflect inside her; she felt herself a creature of the senses, uninhibited and free, the sun's touch an erotic warmth on her bare breasts, the whisper of a strand of hair on her cheek a tickle of the sensual. She closed her eyes again to the glare of sun on water, not asleep and not quite awake, feeling the delicious warmth flood over every inch of her.

She stirred at the sudden cry of a startled bird.

Kern was standing across the pool from her, staring over the rippling silver of the water. His hands were on his hips, his shirt clinging damply to him in the heat.

Dirt was caked on his boots, patched on his jeans; a sheen of sweat glistened in the sun on his forehead. Disheveled, hot, dusty, the bronze of his skin glowed around the physical power of the man, the sheer sexual magnetism only intensified by the moisture on his skin and his disheveled appearance.

She didn't move. Caught and naked beneath his gaze, she felt a vibrant rush of response in her body, a response that only intensified inside as she watched him as he must have watched her.

The shirt was stripped, a broad expanse of golden chest uncaged to the sun. Belt and boots, jeans and briefs . . . she drew in her breath. He waded in the water, and she saw that *all* of his body had a golden tan. His stomach was flat and his thighs pure sinew and the man moved like liquid. He submerged for a moment under the waterfall. His nakedness was so natural in the country he fit so well, a country of predators and prey. Yet it was also a country where the most vulnerable of wildflowers flourished in such gentle profusion . . . images flooded her mind in a wild warm rush. He was wading toward her, his eyes burning.

He reached out a hand while his legs still shimmered in water. "You want to talk, Tish?"

She shook her head. She didn't want to talk. It was all said the moment she took his hand, a sweet whisper of laughter escaping from her at the renewed shock of icy water against her sun-warmed skin. He drew her close, damp hands gliding over her heated body, his mouth blocking out a too-bright sun.

He was wet and shivering cold all over to her baked skin, but the blend was shockingly erotic. His cool lips suddenly heated, claiming hers with a pressure that stole her laughter. The shape of her mouth molded to his, open to the slow curl of his tongue inside, the taste of him filling her until the blend of tastes was the same, no longer hers or his. His palms stroked a silken touch from the nape of her neck down the tapir of her spine, down the gentle round of her hips until his fingertips touched thigh. The second time his hands were less teasingly soft, more deliberately arousing in texture and sensation, and the third time he was kneading her skin to his, forcing her swelling breasts to mold to his chest, forcing her hips to the cradle of his.

The kiss ended when he lifted his head to look at her. Her face was still raised to his. Like smooth warm silk his palms cupped her breasts, his thumbs gently rubbing their tips until she closed her eyes in restless need. Gently the palms smoothed their way up, fingering the delicate arch of collarbone, the hollow of her throat. His kiss followed the same trail as he picked her up.

The pool, the rocks, were brilliant with sun, blinding. The stretch of moss held sun-dappled shade, cool on her back, a grazing sensation that fired new primitive sensations within. The smells were invasive—the sweet white flower she'd never named, the rich pungent moss, Kern's smell of earth and man . . . and her own.

There was fear—of the power of the man which she saw in his smoke-colored eyes. He would possess her. It was the choice she had made, but there was a different flavor knowing she could not take it back. His touch aroused her like the heat and excitement of danger, but the very old fear came with it. What she craved was in his keeping, and her hands suddenly clenched his shoulders, desperate to feel held, protected. And his hands were gentle, soothing, loving, promising. It seemed so easy suddenly.

His flesh was luscious in her hands, filled with vibrant

warmth, blood, life. The beard tickled at her breasts when his mouth loved the hollow of her throat. She writhed, small sounds escaping from her throat. She knew where he wanted touching; she had always known. There had always been a fear of not doing it well, but that fear had no place when everywhere she touched invoked an answering trembling in Kern, an odd pitch in his breathing, his need so sweet, so potent. The song was racing through her veins, out of control. God, Kern, now... "Please..."

"Tell me, Tish," he ordered roughly. "I need to hear you say it's different. I want you to say you couldn't pretend if you tried, couldn't walk away..."

"Please..."

But he was insistently slow, the brush of his beard sweeping her breasts, her stomach, her thighs. He kissed her from her toes to her lips. And it seemed to take a lifetime. The fire kept building inside, lapping at every sense, and there was now a new fear, an almost frantic fear that it would not subside. When his body shifted over hers she clutched at his shoulders, to force him closer.

"Easy, Tish..."

"Love me, Kern."

"Come with me," he murmured. "Come with me, come with me..."

Perhaps the pain was imagined when he pierced through her private core, a sweet pain of promise. Like a virgin's, this one moment was irretrievable. This erased the past. His body controlled hers, taking her higher, closer to flame. Tears burst from her eyes at the same time her body seemed to explode in pleasure...

For an hour they lay together, hands quietly soothing each other after the avalanche of lovemaking. A red squirrel popped from a corner of the thicket to scold, making them laugh. They shifted then—Kern with his back to a tree and Trisha half reclining, her head against his chest and her eyes half closed. A sleepy lethargy seemed to have overtaken her body, yet she was soaring still in the most gentle way from the explosive emotions she'd found for the first time in loving.

"We're going to have to get up, you know." Kern was threading his fingers through her hair in hypnotic fashion.

"Hmmm."

"Although if you continue to lie like that without a stitch on..."

A shy smile touched her lips, but she neither moved nor opened her eyes.

"You know...the Tish I married would never have sun-bathed nude, never have explored such off-the-beaten paths to find a place like this. Five years..." he murmured. "You were loving then and I thought in time the passion would grow. You were so inexperienced, so young...but I never guessed at this kind of hidden fire, at this kind of sexual abandonment."

The words were sweet but Trisha's eyes flickered open, uncertain suddenly at his tone.

"How many have there been, Tish?"

Her head lifted from his lap. "Pardon?"

"Men."

She felt an odd shiver of chill inside, and her throat was suddenly dry—as if she were about to take off on a roller-coaster ride headed downhill. "Do there have to be other men?"

His smoke eyes rested on hers. "From a woman who shied from lights-on at night to wanton in broad daylight? I think it more than likely that men were part of the transition. If you think I'm judging, Tish, I'm not. I find you beautiful, more compelling in passion than any woman I've ever known. And tonight we'll have a bed, not just a stolen moment..."

She drew back almost unconsciously. The urge to cover herself had not been there before, but suddenly it was. She was suddenly aware of bits and pieces of moss clinging to her skin, of a small red graze on her thigh where a stone had scraped, of a heat on her breasts that felt like sunburn.

"You sound to me like you are judging," she said sharply. And the invitation to tonight's bed sounded like an invitation extended to a mistress, not a wife. She stood up and took the few steps to her shorts and halter top still in a heap on the flat white rock. "I never asked if you were celibate for five years, Kern. Though the answer would obviously be no. It wouldn't even have been... healthy if you had. Five years is a long time."

"I only asked you a question. You don't have to answer it. But don't tell me I don't have the right to ask, Tish."

She drew up the shorts, buttoned them. But when she tried to slip on the emerald and navy top, she winced in discomfort.

"You can wear my shirt." He lurched up stiffly to a standing position, preparing to get his own clothes.

"No, thank you." Her head was bent, trying to do the halter straps in a tangle of hair at her neck. Her hands were firmly and suddenly pushed away. He did the straps, smoothed the hair free, and then pulled her back against his bare chest. His arms enfolded her in a sensual cage, his lips pressing into her hair.

"Jealousy feels like hell, Tish, and I spoke before

thinking. *Nothing* matters right now; it wasn't the time to say anything. Smile again for me, bright eyes."

She smiled, and kissed him. But she heard the "right now." The trip down the steep slope was quick. The sun was setting in the west, reminding Trisha of how many hours they had stolen. And of how much had suddenly changed—and how much had not. Everything was right when he was holding her close, but Trisha was all too aware that they walked the last steps separately. Without his arms around her she felt oddly cold, unsure, and in some incomprehensible way, despairing.

8

AT NINE THE dishes were done and the sun was fading. Julia had taken center stage from the moment she walked in a half hour before, oblivious to the odd silence between the two younger Lowerys. The patio at dusk was as cool as anywhere, but the stillness at the end of the day seemed only to intensify the heat wave that nestled in the valley.

"Three fish," Julia repeated for her audience, who were normally more than captive to her every word. "The one fought so hard I found myself in the water, completely ruining my silk pants. I should have worn those horrible jeanish things . . . I saw some deer and wild turkeys, did I tell you that, Kern?"

"Yes."

"I'll have you know I even cooked the fish myself! The kitchen in that mobile home—I swear it's like a doll's setup, everything in miniature. You know how long it's been since I've actually tried to cook anything, but Mr. Michaels . . ." Her monologue trailed off finally, an irritable note in her voice as she darted impatient looks at both of them. "Well, then. Since the two of you are being entirely uncommunicative, I shall retire to my room."

Trisha stood up quickly after Julia. "I'm tired, too. Do you need anything before you go to bed, Julia?"

"I was looking for that antiques magazine this afternoon..."

The women's talk mollified Julia. For Trisha it was an excuse to leave Kern's presence. Once upstairs she closed and locked the door to the bath and turned the taps on full. The tension between them had escalated in each short, uncomfortable little silence. She could not take any more of it.

She stripped off her clothes and slid into the tepid water, sinking to her neck and closing her eyes with a sound of relief. The sunburn in such mortifying places was soothed, cooled. When she emerged half an hour later, she applied an apricot-scented lotion, brushed her hair until it crackled, and drew on an aqua silk nightgown—another of Julia's purchases—that felt better on her overheated skin even than air.

The night was still warm when she stepped from the bathroom, but the sun was long set. Her room was the color of dusk, and the man on her bed blended in shadow until he stood up the moment she opened the door.

Kern's hand grasped hers, persuasively firm as he walked her down the hall to his room—to their own room. He only let go of her hand when he had shut the door with both of them inside.

"You're tired, Tish. So am I."

A dare to start an argument if ever she'd heard one. His look was granite. He started taking off his clothing in the semidarkness, as if it were settled between them. Obviously he did not intend to sleep alone tonight. She debated for a moment about pitting the wildflower fragility she felt inside to his mountain granite, and came up with the obvious conclusion.

Slowly she unfolded the spread and laid it on the chair and then quietly slid in between the cool sheets. Kern was done with his shirt and removed his pants.

"Were you actually planning on sleeping in the spare room tonight?" he asked finally.

She swallowed the developing lump in her throat. "You didn't ask me to stay," she said quietly.

"It shouldn't need to be said." His voice grated and then became gentle like velvet teasing her in the darkness. "Tish, you're sunburned and you're tired. I know that. We don't have to make love. I just want you here, sleeping next to me—"

She drew in her breath. "That wasn't what I meant, Kern. You haven't asked me to . . . *stay,"* she said softly. "This afternoon . . ." Her pride was battered because she had to ask. At the waterfall, it hadn't mattered. She had told herself she only wanted that moment, not knowing or caring how he felt about her. She had thought it would be enough. It was a sad lie to have told herself . . .

He drew back the sheet and slipped in beside her, bolstering the pillow behind him. The scent and warmth of him were suddenly there, clean and male and potent, but he made no move to touch her. His voice was gentle but she could feel fear licking all up and down her spine.

"You're here, Tish. That's your choice. I could have come after you when you left the first time, but I didn't then and I wouldn't now. I swore I'd never ask you to stay again. It was done the first time, when I gave you that ring still on your finger. That 'once' said all I had to say."

"I hear you," she said softly, and turned on her side in the darkness. The hurt was sudden, swift, and painful.

It never occurred to her that there might be another interpretation of his words. She heard only what she was really expecting to hear. He would never ask her to stay because he had really never wanted her back, not as a wife again. As long as she was here, of course, her own behavior had given him license to make love with her. But as far as her staying . . . it was not his choice. She was not surprised his love had died. There was no blame for Kern, only the anguished wish that she had never come.

Wet eyes dried in the darkness. A long time later Kern half stirred in sleep, one leg draping over hers, his arm cradled between her breasts. A breeze coaxed in coolness, the special quiet of a mountain night. The last of her mountain nights, she thought fleetingly. She suddenly wished that she'd told Kern how she saw him as a lover. Sensitive, fierce, gentle. It seemed terribly important to tell him that it wasn't his fault she had not responded a long time ago . . . it was important, because she knew there would be no other time.

Impeded by the weight of Kern's arm on her hip, she half sat up in the darkness, pulling off her nightgown. Her breasts felt hot and tender after the afternoon's exposure to the sun. Crushed against his chest they felt painful, but an erotic pain that she welcomed. Her palm slowly skimmed over his sleep-warmed flesh, down his side and hips, back up over his taut buttocks and spine.

He half turned in sudden restless sleep. She slid lower, so that her lips were on a level with his heart. One of her slim legs tangled between his, holding him close as she sought to give him some of the love he had once so freely offered her. She hadn't contemplated waking or even arousing him. She only wished to express what she had failed so badly to express before: his body was beautiful to her. She simply wanted him to know. Her lips grazed the warm skin of his chest, from the flat male nipples hidden in a curling matt of hair to the smoother flesh that covered his ribs. His skin was like warm satin.

"Tish . . ."

She reached up, her fingertips brushing his lips to silence him. His mouth was so soft next to the grainy texture of beard and her fingers explored the angle of his cheekbone, the shape of his broad forehead. Gently, slowly, she kissed each of his eyes closed again, and then crouched over him, trailing patterns of kisses, memorizing his throat and shoulders, his ribs and stomach. A fever started to consume her. A fever brought on by the darkness and silence, the feel and scent of his body. Her breasts burned and she felt light-headed. Perhaps it was just knowing he had wakened, yet when his palm slowly slid from her nape to the curve of her sun-heated breast, she flinched—not in rejection, but in almost painful, intense sensitivity. Not even that afternoon had desire been so compelling, so fierce.

Her hand kneaded restlessly, up and down his thigh. And Kern made a sudden deep growling sound from the bottom of his throat. He had been so obediently still, but no more. He opened his eyes before his mouth touched hers, then he rose and pressed her down on to the cool sheets. His hands felt like fire on her breasts, sweeping urgently down her ribs and stomach. Her whole body contracted as he caressed her thighs. Her hands clutched his hair and from her throat came a long low sound of pain. *Love me, Kern*, she wanted to cry. *I can't bear leaving you. Not now.*

He was inside her before she could draw breath, her startled cry of pleasure blending with his. She wanted to obliterate every other thought but him, lose herself in their lovemaking. It was as if he knew how she felt. He rolled onto his back so she could be on top. He raised his head to lick at her sunburned breasts. But in the next instant she was beneath him again, his hands holding her hair, while his tongue parodied the loveplay of their bodies. Finally, side by side, his palms cupped her bottom, urging her legs to fold around him. He whispered low, husky encouragements, urging a wanton response from her she hadn't known she possessed. She heard Kern's gutteral cry just when the fever exploded inside her body in a long low rush.

He held her then, soothing her, his kisses gentle on her damp cheeks, in her hair. "So beautiful, Tish..." He held her long after they were both still, long after she finally heard the sound of his even breathing again. He held her as if he would never let her go.

"Patricia! This is the most ridiculous thing I've ever heard of! You can't simply take off like this. Put those things *down* and talk to me!" Julia stormed, snatching at the navy-and-emerald shorts on the bed that Trisha was not planning to take anyway. Trisha stood back erect from the suitcase, and sighed.

"I love you, Julia," she said patiently, soothingly. "And Kern loves you as well. When you're back north I'll come and see you again, just as I've always done. Please don't be upset."

"You keep talking about *me*. I want to talk about *you*. Where is my son this morning?" Julia demanded fretfully.

"He'll be back by lunch. He's out with Matt. They're checking out areas where dead trees have to be cut down. Normally they'd let them fall in the natural way, but with the weather so dry there's the threat of forest fires—"

"I don't give a hoot about all that!" Julia said snappishly.

"Well, you should. Kern does," Trisha said wryly. She closed the suitcase with a snap and lifted it. The case was bulging. What wouldn't fit in had been boxed and was already put away in the attic.

"You had an argument," Julia said, probing. "You must have. You were both quiet last evening. But I thought everything was going fine—"

"Everything is fine," Trisha said quietly and set down the case yet again to reach out and hug the older lady. "You would have liked it to turn out differently, I know that. I'm sorry, darling. But I can't help..." His words had echoed through the long night, and settled that morning after he'd left: *I swore I'd never ask you to stay again...that 'once' said all I had to say...*

"At least stay until lunch. You're looking too tired for that long drive, Patricia." Julia trailed her down the stairs, through the kitchen, out the back door. Trisha set her suitcase on the back seat, reached up to readjust a pin at the back of her neat chignon, and settled in the driver's seat. The rest of Julia's monologue she had blocked out. She had the sudden realization that she hadn't the money to make the trip. She'd spent it on the outfit she'd worn the day they had picked up Julia from the hospital. The mauve pantsuit she wore today.

"Are you even listening to me?" Julia asked plaintively.

Trisha looked up from her wallet. There was a lone Gulf credit card. Could she make the entire journey on Gulf gas stations? She looked up at Julia, knowing she no longer felt free to ask for help. "No, I wasn't listening, darling. My mind's made up. Kern is not going to be upset, Julia; he is going to be furious for about an hour and a half, and then you're going to find he's completely relieved that I'm gone. There is nothing for you to worry about. Did you take your pills this morning?"

"I swear, if I'd raised you you wouldn't have been able to sit down regularly!" Julia said, sputtering helplessly.

"Did you?" Trisha insisted.

"Yes."

"Good. I know you're upset. Just go in and put your feet up and relax. Right now. Or for the next four election years you'll see me actively campaigning for the liberal party, Julia—"

The fleeting look of horror that transformed Julia's features broke up her frantic monologue. She stiffened, expelling an exasperated breath. "Patricia, that is *not* amusing."

"No," Trisha said wearily. "Nothing is really amusing this morning. Please, darling . . ."

She slipped on dark glasses as she backed up and turned the car down the drive. A few more minutes and Trisha would be off his land, and she was suddenly desperate to be gone. Distance would give her a better perspective. Had it really only been three weeks? Three weeks ago she had no more illusions of getting back with Kern than she would have had hope of growing wings . . .

Hikers trailed the side of the road; she could not drive quickly. And then there was Jack, his blond head shining in the sun, his arm motioning her over to stop when he caught sight of the car. And she stopped, her features masked in a polite smile as Jack approached.

"Have you seen Kern?"

She shook her head. "I think he's out with Matt."

"Well, if you run into him, Trisha, would you tell him to hightail it down to the camp?"

Her lips opened, parting to ask what was wrong, if there was anything she could help with. And closed, not liking at all the concerned frown on Jack's normally smooth forehead, but not having any choice except to ignore it. "I'll be gone," she said carefully. "If you need to get ahold of him, you might leave a message up with his mother."

"Oh, well . . . have a good day!"

It wasn't. It was a perfectly wretched day. It was $5.57 of fast-food hamburgers and searching out Gulf stations. It was a day of blinding sunshine that glared like a headache and congested cities where the heat seemed to mushroom down in the traffic. A poor excuse for a sunset brought a measure of relief from the heat as she crossed the state border into Ohio, but if there were any flatter states, she didn't know them. Ohio was one long straight black ribbon of road on a night that held no stars. No one else seemed to be driving in the wee hours. Just black sky, black road, black mood . . . and despite exhaustion, her nerves were still stretched fragile and taut.

Five o'clock in the morning brought Trisha to the outskirts of Detroit—and the company. Motor City would have taken personal offense if its highways were empty. The rush hour never ended in the center of town. She merged into the flow as she had thousands of times in the last five years, familiar with Detroit's dusty skyline at dawn. The heartbeat of the city—the cloverleafs of highway piled one on top of the other, the noise and rush, action and excitement, thousands of faces with no names—it was all familiar, and a last shot of adrenalin speeded obediently in her veins. All she had to do was convince herself that she belonged here again . . .

And you *do*, she told herself. Everything you've built

on your own is here. You have friends and a good job you worked hard for...But the inner pep talk had too much of a hollow ring to it. She stopped trying. In an hour she had passed by the four-by-one-mile elitist concentration of power and money that was Grosse Pointe; five minutes from there the car was parked and she was striding up the walk to her town house, dragging her suitcase in one hand with her key in the other.

The apartment was small and attractive from the outside, with dark-olive siding and a sloping lawn that looked manicured. The promise of privacy was what had led her to sign the lease in the first place; the complex was shielded by a tall brick wall. For the first time it struck her how ironic it was, that in the city one measured privacy in fences...in the mountains it was simply there, free, something one found inside, and outside as well.

She slipped her key in the lock and turned it, nearly tripping over the pile of mail that had accumulated by the door in her absence. The pink and gold of her living room accented the feminine furniture. Her choices, so carefully and slowly accumulated over the years, always gave her pleasure when she walked in. But at the moment the air was stifling, dusty, and stale, and the silence only spelled out a terrible kind of loneliness. Trisha set down her suitcase, almost dizzy from exhaustion, slipped off her shoes in the middle of the room, and weaved to the bedroom.

She threw open the windows for air, heard the blare of a dozen traffic horns, and closed them again. Not yet—she really couldn't cope with the city yet. The heat didn't matter. Nothing mattered. She drew down the leaf-green spread, trying again to take just a moment of pleasure in what was familiar. The bedroom held white wicker furniture with fabrics in leaf-green and white; cool and fresh, it had always pleased. The indifference that she felt inside jarred, as if she had been betrayed by something she had counted on to sustain her. You're just tired, she told herself as she stripped off the pantsuit and crashed on the mattress.

Her eyes fluttered open once to set the alarm. Three things had to be done before night. She had to go to the bank and retrieve money from her savings. And food. There wasn't any, of course, in the apartment. And last . . . a lawyer. It was five years past time, but suddenly even hours seemed too long to wait.

The alarm was set for one-thirty in the afternoon. Her hand fell limp on the mattress seconds after she set it.

"No, I don't have an appointment," Trisha admitted to the sleekly groomed redhead with efficient eyes. She'd never met anyone before who could be said to have efficient eyes. "I've met Mr. Whitaker before; he'll know who I am. I would appreciate it if you would at least give him my name."

Cal Whitaker emerged from his office moments later, oblivious to his secretary's sniff of disapproval at the obvious break from appointment protocol. "Patricia Lowery! What brings you to lawyer's row? Nice to see you, sweetheart!"

Pin-striped, with a brown tie, Cal was a long lanky man who had little claim to good looks and a lot to distinguished ones—mustache, pipe, silver sideburns, Savile Row suits . . . and a come-on in the brown eyes that Trisha had had the occasion to turn down a long time ago.

She stood up, receiving his hand and second-thought kiss on the cheek with a cool smile. Cal's appraisal certainly reaffirmed that the lemon linen dress could distract from the heavy circles beneath her eyes.

"A social call, I certainly hope?"

Trisha shook her head, being led into the dark paneled office ahead of him. "I need your professional services."

"Well, we can take care of anything, gorgeous."

She winced a little when he winked. The chair she settled in was living-room comfortable, and a glass of wine was served—part of the office decor was his bar. A dozen buttons were on his desk. He had turned three shelves of the bookcase into the bar. She felt no curiosity about the others. He was a country-club sort of lawyer who did that sort of job very well.

"I need a divorce, Cal. From your reputation, perhaps your schedule is full, but since I know you, I thought I'd ask—"

"I'd have been offended if you hadn't." He smiled warmly, received no answering warm smile in return, and set down his glass. From his pocket he drew out a pair of wire-rims, dropped the banter, and unearthed a clean legal pad from his desk. "I'm sorry to hear you're having trouble," he said more formally. "Why don't you just start by telling me how things stand at the moment."

She stared at him woodenly. "There isn't anything to tell. I just want a divorce."

He smiled gently. "So you said. A very rough time for everyone involved, but we do have to start somewhere. Grounds, Patricia? Obviously you're the one who wants to file."

"Yes." Cal had the practice of a mother who hands out Band-Aids to her toddler. He didn't really want to hear the same old story of how the hurt came to be any more than she had any intention of telling him, but somehow—ridiculously—it never occurred to her that she would actually have to talk to him. She didn't want to talk. She just wanted it done.

And as for grounds? Was she supposed to be able to stand up and say that Kern didn't love her?

"Patricia?"

She swallowed the unforgivable urge to cry. "Isn't there a no-fault divorce law in Michigan? Where both people simply agree—"

"Yes, of course. If that's the situation."

"How long does it take?"

"Well, that depends, Patricia. If there are no children—"

She felt a ridiculous urge to cry. "There are no children."

"And if everyone agrees readily on a property settlement—"

She shook her head. "There won't be any problem. There's no property involved. I don't want alimony or anything else from my . . . husband."

Cal's pencil touched tip to desk, then eraser. Back and forth. Flip-flop. His eyes regarded her patiently, his lawyer's mind spinning out the potential state of his client as it affected his fee. Finally he drawled, "We all tend to react rather quickly when our feelings are involved, Patricia. I see a lot of it. It's the name of the game in divorce. My father was Ralph Lowery's attorney, did you know that?"

"Yes." Julia had told her once, and indirectly it was how she had met Cal before. He was a Grosse Pointe neighbor of sorts.

"I may not still have call to know the personal circumstances of your husband these days, Patricia, but anyone on our side of town is familiar with the Lowery estate. As a wife you're entitled to your fair share, if only to ease some of the trauma of the divorce itself. And there's your future to think of. It's my job to—"

"No."

"You don't have to be involved, honey. This kind of thing is done directly between lawyer's offices. You can trust me to take care of your interests, Patricia—"

She stood up rapidly, a hunted-doe look in her eyes as sudden nausea wrenched in her stomach. "I don't want that. I don't want any of that. All I want is to sign a piece of paper, Cal. Can't you just—"

"Patricia, have you really talked this over with your husband?"

"There will be no argument from Kern. But he might try . . . I don't want his money. There's no reason for this to be any more complicated, I just . . ."

The tears gushed then, mortifyingly free in front of this man who was undoubtedly used to overemotional women in his office. With practiced patience he had his handkerchief just as ready as the wine. But this wasn't just any divorce, she wanted to cry out. Don't you understand how much I love my husband? Don't you understand that if I thought he *really* wanted me . . .

"Now, now, Patricia. Don't be embarrassed. We'll have all this settled before you know it; it'll hardly take any time at all. We'll celebrate with a dinner out when it's all over, when it's all behind you. We'll wait to discuss the fee another time. I'll get everything in the mill; don't you worry about a thing . . ."

It was seven before she could make it back to her apartment, loaded down with two bags of groceries, feeling as if she hadn't slept in a year. With the food put away, she slipped into the shower, cleansing off the city grit of a warm afternoon. Clad in a loose silk kimono, thigh-length, she wandered barefoot back to the kitchen, opening the refrigerator now full, seeing nothing she really wanted, though a bowl of raspberries seemed— possible. Her stomach was in knots. Her nerves were frayed. The tears kept feeling like they were just behind her eyes, still trying to burst out, and she was more than disgusted with herself that they already had in Cal's office.

The worst of it was that she knew she was waiting for the telephone to ring. Kern would have long since realized she was gone. If there was any chance he still wanted her back, he would have called. Every time she turned around she was imagining him there, just arrived, imagining what he would look like as he walked around her apartment for the first time.

"Very pretty, Tish, but there isn't a stick of furniture a man my size could get comfortable in." With the dish of raspberries in her hand, she surveyed with a different eye her pink-and-gold living room, coming up with the same dissatisfied feeling.

"But you've really done well for yourself. You really made it completely on your own, didn't you, bright eyes?" And her heart swelled, knowing she had done well, that she was a woman now and not a child, capable of handling her own life. It was no longer as an appendage of Kern that she saw herself.

She set down the ridiculous dish of raspberries, curled up on the couch, and put her head in her hands. "I like the robe, Tish. Silk like your skin..." The memory of their loving by the waterfall twisted inside; she could feel her breasts swell in desire even now, the look in his eyes, the panther grace of the naked man...

Stop it, she told herself. And stared at the telephone,

knowing he was not going to call. She had left him once and he had never come after her. He had said as much. She knew it, in her heart. There had been no words of love, only passion.

She napped erratically on the couch, and when she woke again at ten-thirty her body was protesting her sporadic eating habits, insisting she find something to sustain it. She fixed a sandwich finally, switched on the news, and settled back on the couch.

The announcer was the newer breed of newscaster, flamboyant in dress, with a personal air. He was enthusiastic about a satellite flight, depressed about one of Congress's latest bills, lurid about a national kidnapping scandal. Trisha only half listened, munching the sandwich as she threaded through the pile of mail that had been at her door.

". . . only a spark. But the weather's been so dry and hot in the Smokies that that was all it took . . ."

She dropped the letter in her hand and bounded up to raise the volume on the TV set.

". . . park service people have their hands full trying to control the rapidly vacating populice in the Smokies, though the fire hasn't spread that far. Fire officials claim there'll be no problem, that the blaze won't get as far east as the national park and for vacationers not to panic. It's still the biggest blaze they've had in over forty years, old-time residents tell us; and in the meantime, Jimmy Barker and his six-year-old son Robert are dead . . ."

"Now in Tiger Town . . ."

Frantically Trisha switched to another station, whose newscaster was just as interested in baseball scores, and switched to a third who was still waxing poetic on the satellite success before he enthused over the city's team.

The Smokies were only worth a sixty-second spot where local interest might have been spurred in the vacation season. Trisha stood, feeling a frustration like rage building inside when no amount of dial-twisting was going to tell her any more. The two dead, but how many were hurt? And west of the Smokies was Kern's. If he wasn't hurt, no one would be able to keep him out of it. And his land, his mountain that he loved so, everything he had worked for... and Julia.

With her head throbbing, she reached for the telephone, but neither the news stations nor the newspapers had any other information to impart. There was a fire. Two people had died. The blaze wasn't over yet but it was now considered "in control," and there was no list of injuries. Perhaps on tomorrow's news...

She paced the living room, then finally gave in and picked up the telephone again to dial long distance. The operator was pleasant, but informed her that many lines were down in that area and those in operation were for emergency use only. Did she have an emergency?

"No—I—thank you." She hung up, hugging her arms to her breasts. No, she didn't have an emergency. In fact, the afternoon had been wretchedly spent severing all ties with the man. They didn't have a marriage. She no longer even had the right to ask.

With a disgusted sound in her throat, she reached one last time for the telephone, arranging for a plane ticket to Knoxville and a rental car from there. In five minutes she was pulling things from her closet, scolding herself in a raging inner tirade that wouldn't quit. Someone would be doing her a kindness to come in and simply put a straight jacket on her. What did she think she was going to do in a fire? Did she have any illusions that there was actually anyone who would allow her within miles of it? And in emergencies too many bystanders always crowded in. The sensible thing to do was wait and see, stay out of the way. And if she did find him— what was she supposed to say? I know I just left you, Kern, I even applied for the divorce papers this afternoon, but . . .

But what, Tish, she told herself sarcastically. Yet the clothes kept filling the suitcase and the robe she wore was in a heap on the floor, replaced by a simple pair of light brown pants and gold-yolked shirt, a brown, gold and orange scarf on her hair. She paused in front of the mirror, seeing the mascara wand in her hand as if it were a stranger's. Getting made up to go to a fire? But the hand kept moving—mascara, blush, lipstick. She was running on instincts and they were stronger than any rational argument she was capable of.

Fifteen miles away from Kern's and there was the smell of forest burning. There were no billowing clouds of smoke but an increasingly pervasive haze that made the air difficult to breathe, as if something heavy were trying to force its way into her lungs. She stepped out when she stopped the car for gas. The atmosphere in the cloying heat had a tension to it, a brooding stillness. No birds were singing, no branches rustling in the surrounding woodlands. Fear paralyzed her for a moment as she got back in the rented car again, and then she felt a kind of desperate calm.

Each mile increased her determination to find him. She braked once, backed up to where she could see between two crevices in the cliffs; in the far distance was smoke, the beginnings of a ravaged forest. People, like brown-uniformed ants, were walking around bare tree trunks, and even from where she had stopped there was the sickeningly sweet smell of new ash. The sun blazed cruelly down on that glimpse of hillside, showing off stark, pitiful destruction.

She drove on, the rock face too high for several miles on both sides to see anything. That desperate calm had suddenly clotted inside her. The instinct to reach Kern, see him, know he was all right, was like a monumental force that surpassed any other emotion.

About five miles from Kern's, a brown-uniformed ranger guarded a makeshift roadblock. Sweat was pouring from his brow as he marched the few steps to lean on her windshield. "We're diverting traffic to another route, miss. I'm afraid there's been some road damage up ahead, trees and rocks down. If you just turn around and head south about two miles, we've mapped out an alternative route—"

She interrupted him. "My husband is Kern Lowery." Suddenly her throat was so dry she could hardly get the words out. "Our home is just ahead a few miles. If you by any chance . . . if you know . . ."

Compassion touched the dark brown eyes of the officer when the question faltered on her lips. "Sure, ma'am. Last I knew he was fine. Known Kern for a few years, I have. Fire tickled his northern slope, I hear, but it jumped on by him for the most part. You must have been away?"

"Yes. Can I get through? I *have* to get through! I could walk from here—"

"It's just not safe, ma'am," He shook his head sympathetically. "And there'll be road crews that don't need a car in the way, neither. It's not like you'd be likely to find your husband home, ma'am. Everybody around here has been helpin' as they could. The damage—" He shook his head sadly. "Well, we help each other around here.

We always have. People been workin' around the clock for some thirty, forty, hours now—"

"Is it finally out? I saw some smoke a while back—"

"Smoldering mostly. There's a few places still blazing, but the flames finally tuckered out."

"There must be camps set up. Coffee and food for the men working—"

He nodded, "All over the place. Down the road a mile is one—"

"I can get to that then?"

The ranger adjusted his hat to scratch his balding head, squinting in that direction. "I don't rightly know. Jeeps have been getting through, of course, four-wheeled-drive vehicles—"

"I can get through," Trisha said firmly and restarted her car.

9

STUMBLING A LITTLE awkwardly on the rocky path, Trisha crested the rise and stopped. The camp was chaos: three makeshift tents with army-cot beds, kerosene burners where huge coffee pots steamed in the middle of the sun, a pair of Red Cross jeeps. There was one long picnic table where some twenty people or so were eating, and another table where two men were standing making sandwiches, their fingers like fan blades in ceaseless motion.

Each face had the same story to tell: physical and mental exhaustion. Soot-stained foreheads, ripped clothes, a mixture of uniforms and bejeanned locals, a few with bandages in one place or another that gleamed white against the general grime of everyone's person. Trisha let out her breath when she was certain Kern was not among them. For another full sixty seconds she stood surveying the scene, unnoticed, and then she strode forward and rolled up her sleeves.

At dusk a new shift of women came. Trisha barely noticed. The why, when, or how of people coming and

going was long irrelevant by then. There was always a
reason. Hunger, rest, transportation, first aid. Very little
talking went on because no one had that kind of energy,
and after six hours Trisha knew she looked no different
than anyone else—vacant-eyed, exhausted, dirt-smudged,
harassed by mosquitoes. It didn't matter. It was two hours
after that before the workers were assured the seige was
over. The fire was well and truly out and it was just a
question now of hauling in the people involved. Trisha
was refilling a heavy pot of coffee with both hands when
she felt a hand on her shoulder. She whirled, "Kern" on
her lips before she even saw who it was.

"Sorry, not Kern," Rhea said with a wry tone that
was not without compassion. "He'll be here in an hour
or two from now, I should think. Do you know I've been
working next to you for over half an hour without even
recognizing you?"

Trisha smiled ruefully in greeting, wiping a damp
strand of hair from her forehead. "There's hardly been
time to worry about looks," she admitted. "He's all right?"

Rhea, setting out cups in front of her so that Trisha
could pour, looked at her curiously. "Well, you've probably seen him since I have. I caught two minutes of him
this morning when he got a spot of breakfast here. Said
hello to him and had my head bitten off—not that we're
not all tired. But he wasn't talking to anybody, like he
was fighting his own personal war."

Trisha frowned. It didn't sound like Kern, who was
always cool in a crisis. And obviously from her comments Rhea was unaware she had left, so it was all the
more awkward to try and talk. "I don't know the last
time you saw Julia," she said, probing carefully.

Rhea laughed. "She is something, isn't she? So determined not to leave, you could have heard her in Cal-

ifornia yesterday afternoon. But the Carolina coast's only a couple of hours drive, and that professor from the camp looked like more than a good Joe. A full week on the ocean and everything will be back to normal around here, Kern had said."

So Kern had packed Julia off with Mr. Matthews, out of harm's way and in safekeeping. Her heart was suddenly singing. They were all right, both of them...

Rhea moved off and Trisha switched jobs. The drinks were poured but the last mountain of sandwiches, almost impossibly, was gone again. It was time to make more. Someone set a lantern down on her table, a beacon of welcoming light as the night darkened.

Her hands kept moving but the smile on her face suddenly stilled. All right. She knew almost for certain that he was well; she was not nearly as certain that she could actually face him. It would be altogether easier on both of them for her to just slip away again...

"Hey, sweetheart, we have any more sugar stored anywhere?"

Sugar and dry cream. It hadn't taken even the first hour to know where supplies were stored.

Well, in a while she would go. She was caught up in the scene, the tales of horror and the tales of heroism, the faces so exhausted, laughter without complaining, a community caught up in its cause. The discomforts were mounting: mosquitoes and aching limbs, the smoke smell burning in her eyes after so many hours of it, sticking clothes and light-headedness from sheer exhaustion. But there was joy too, at being needed. It was her cause, her country, too.

"One more group coming in. Should be the last. Hey, has anybody looked straight up recently? Clouds!"

And there were restless white-gray swirling patterns

low in the night sky. Trisha's hands served a dozen more makeshift dinners, but her face kept flickering up. A breeze suddenly whispered through the camp, tossing up a paper cup and sending it soaring.

"That has to be the last group," Rhea said wearily from behind her. "And it's nearly midnight, high time. I didn't see Kern, Trisha. You want to ride out with me?"

"No, I'm fine. But thanks, Rhea."

Only a half dozen people were left after that to handle the last of the cleanup. The Red Cross cleared out and the tents were being taken down; paper plates and cups had to be stacked in boxes, the food organized. A sudden gust of wind brought the first hint of dampness—and a joyous shout from one of the men. Rain would destroy the last threat of fire, bring relief from the heat and oppressive haze; they all understood.

The sky seemed to hesitate, and then it happened. Drip to sprinkle to spray to downpour. Trisha dropped the folded blanket in her hands and was helplessly caught up in the laughter of the rest. From adults with weighty responsibilities one minute to children the next—they were all the same, punch-drunk tired, arms spread wide to embrace the rain, tongues out to lap up the taste.

Trisha's blouse soaked to her skin, the cool liquid dribbling down her neck, down her breasts. Her hair was matted to dark gold, her face raised to the dark sky for the blessed freshness. Like silk on her skin, just like silk. The others forgotten, she inhaled the new fresh air, her eyes closed in sheer sensual enjoyment . . .

The fingers that clenched her arms bit. Trisha's eyes blinked open, lashes too matted with rain and mascara even to see. Her heart lurched, recognizing Kern.

His shirt gaped almost to the waist, smudged with soot and grime and torn. He smelled of sweat and smoke, and Trisha had never seen such hollows beneath his eyes, such a white pallor of exhaustion beneath his tan. The rain pelting down matted his hair; even his beard and shaggy brows were dripping. Black coals for eyes seared down to her face and the fingers clenching her shoulders half shook her. *"What* are you doing here?"

She drew back, almost frightened by the towering rage that vibrated from him.

"Don't you pull that trembling act with me! If I had you alone right now—"

"Kern . . ." Her voice was soft to his roar. She had expected anger when he saw her again and perhaps she was even prepared for it. But that was hours before, when she wasn't limb-aching tired, emotionally strung out herself. The rain kept streaming down on both of them, but what a moment ago was blessedly cool now chilled. Soaked, wary, exhausted, Trisha trembled and raised her hands to release his from her shoulders.

"We ready to get moving, Kern?" someone called out from behind them.

"Right now," Kern snapped back, but he was still staring at Trisha. Her eyes flickered, scanning his features for any sign of tenderness, but the dark night and rain blurred his expression.

"You have to drive the others," she said awkwardly.

"Everyone who's left." His hand on her shoulder slid down to her wrist, his grip so tight that it bit into her tender skin. She shivered again, holding back when he tried to pull her behind him.

"I'm not coming, Kern. I didn't walk here. I rented a car. Just—"

"Don't bother. You must be basket-case tired if you think you're getting away like that."

"No—"

"I'm too damned tired to argue." His mouth silenced her with raw emotion that bruised her like a punishment as he picked her up. She was viced to his chest so tightly she could hardly breathe, a fire of protest and panic racing through her bloodstream as he strode toward the jeep with her.

Enthusiastic catcalls greeted them from the five men packed inside, even more enthusiastic when she was all but threaded through the opening and deposited onto a variety of male laps in the back, deserted while Kern vaulted into the driver's seat.

The ride was a nightmare. A Ray and a John identified themselves; the rest of the names she didn't catch. The rain kept pouring down on the canvas top to the jeep and the air was all but steaming from the packed damp bodies in such a close space. She couldn't balance without touching someone's thigh or stomach, and the four men packed in the back with her were just as exhausted as they were momentarily boisterous, teasing the lone lady in their midst. They'd have to share her, they said. And then it was thank God she was just a bit of a package, and Kern, how did he manage at night with such a squirmer?

The jeep was finally braked in front of the neon signs of a motel in Gatlinburg. Kern grabbed up the keys and finally looked back at her. "You're going to keep her safe for me for a moment, boys?"

"We decided to keep her, period," one of the men quipped and the others laughed. Kern, expressionless, simply strode off into the motel office and returned a few minutes later to hand the room key to the man sitting in the passenger seat. "I took care of your transportation in the morning, ten o'clock. And breakfast's on the house. It's only one room, but there'll be extra blankets. You guys can make do." His words were clipped, and then the others were rapidly unfolding from the jeep, following the lead of the first from the passenger seat.

The last hesitated. "Kern, I thought you were coming with us. There's still no power beyond the valley, is there? And the roads weren't clear..."

"We'll manage," Kern said curtly. "Just go on, get out of the rain. Get some rest. We all need it." When the door closed and the last of the men were racing for the cover of their room, Kern turned back to Trisha, huddled and shivering in the back seat. "Get up here, Tish."

She crawled forward obediently, not willing to be bounced any more than she had to be in the crude back compartment, too tired to argue anyway, and wordlessly grateful she did not have to pass the night in a room with the five other men. It didn't take much intelligence to gather that there were simply no rooms left in the valley. Emergency accommodations only stretched so far in the thinly populated area, and the rain would have made it that much worse.

She glanced at Kern as he started the engine and put the jeep in gear. Her arms were huddled across her chest from the increasing chill of damp clothes, but the real shivering came from inside. Her nerves felt like rubber-bands, stretched to the breaking point, an absolute wretchedness that was beyond tears and beyond trying to calm herself down rationally. There'd been three days of stress and high-powered emotions, and she simply couldn't cope with anything more.

He didn't talk. He glanced at her once and switched on the heater, his face almost gray-white under the few streetlights they passed. They passed through the town and started the familiar climb of the mountain road. It was less than half an hour before they came to the spot where she had parked her rented car. It seemed a year.

"Kern..."

He must have seen it too, for his answer was rapid and his speed didn't alter. "We're going home. If I were you, I wouldn't argue."

It wasn't that. In her car were clothes and her purse—and she looked back, watching the little red car disappear when they rounded the curve. And then just ahead there was a barricade where rocks had fallen. Kern stopped the car and she saw his figure by headlights pushing aside the barrier so they could get through. A huge rock had tumbled in the road along with other debris; the jeep vaulted over them obediently, cocked just for one minute at a tilted angle that made her clutch the seat for balance.

They had just cleared that and turned a curve when Kern jammed on the brakes, throwing a hand in front of her to keep Trisha from falling forward. "Damn it," he murmured as he slammed out of the vehicle again. It was a tree this time, stretched too far across the road for him to get over or around. She saw again his towering figure in the headlights trying to push the bulky obstruction, and something—finally—calmed inside. With a flick back of her hair she opened her door and ran out to help him, the rain drenching her all over again.

"Get back in there!" Kern shouted at her.

She paid no attention, trying to see in the darkness what they had to do. The trunk of the tree wasn't so very large, but it was tall, and the little mountain of wet black branches seemed insurmountable, far too heavy to actually move for two or even four people. But they didn't have to move it, just get around it... if they wanted to get home. And Trisha felt a momentum inside that brooked no other rational thought: she was going to get home.

Kern was pulling from the opposite side and Trisha waded in to help, involuntarily calling out when a rough sharp branch caught and scratched at her side.

"If you get hurt, I'm going to darned well murder you, Tish!"

"That was the intention anyway, wasn't it, Kern? To murder me when we get home?" she shouted back. "Why don't you tell me what to do instead of just glowering at me?"

Gasping, breathless, fifteen minutes later she raced back again for the cover of the jeep with Kern just beside her. When she slammed the door she reached with both hands to lift the heavy weight of drenched hair from her face, but there was exhilaration in her expression. They had managed to move enough debris to get through, and Kern beside her sat a ridiculously long minute just looking at her before he started the jeep again. There was just a twist of an unwilling smile guarded in that dark beard, the first she had seen since he'd found her, but it was there.

"You look like absolute hell!" he said, growling.

"Next time I'll wear something more appropriate for a fire," she promised lightly.

He started the jeep. "Pardon?"

"Nothing, Kern. I don't understand what all of this is about—why everything's in the road—"

"A good-sized fire makes its own wind; trees start crashing into trees. There can even be an earthquake effect if it's a good enough blaze. This one, thank God, wasn't that bad. But bad enough."

So it was not impossible, then, to talk for two and a half seconds. She closed her eyes and huddled down in the seat for the last of the ride, finally almost too tired to care that she was soaked and cold and frightened. She was not wanted and he was still angry, and she hadn't even an inkling of an idea how she was going to cope, the thread of her heartbeat saying she simply couldn't.

When the jeep stopped again her eyes flickered open. They were home. No lights shone from the shadowed house and there was no sign of life, but the rain was finally dwindling to sporadic sprinkles, and the clouds shifting above were letting through the light of a crescent moon. She felt a sense of relief so intense that she simply closed her eyes for a moment, her limbs finally feeling like dead weight, and she was barely aware that Kern had gotten out until the passenger door opened beside her.

Obediently she turned her legs out, and just as obediently she told her mind to unfold the rest of her body, to get out and walk. All systems balked inside, as though to say, sorry, Tish, we've just had enough. Large hands suddenly reached in and pulled her out, and for one insane minute she felt her forehead suspended to his chest as if that were her only contact with reality.

"You're worse than a basket case!"

"You can't hit a lady when she's down," Trisha murmured vaguely. Limbs like water were shifted and she found herself carried again, unable to protest, her eyes insisting on staying closed. She was dipped down so that his hand could reach the door handle, and then they were out of the endless moisture, dry, warm, and close in the back hall. He set her tentatively on her feet, one arm still supporting her under her shoulder. "If you can stand for just a minute, Tish, I can get a lantern. We're out of power at least until tomorrow..."

"Of course," she murmured, "I'm perfectly fine."

It sounded good, but the moment his arms left her her knees promptly buckled. Before she could fall she was swooped up again.

"They don't seem to work," she told him, apologizing faintly.

"You're making it damned difficult, Tish," he murmured in her ear. "You know damn well I still feel like murdering you." But it really no longer sounded that way. And it really no longer felt that way as he carried her blindly through the house, groping at doorways up the completely black darkness of the stairway. His grip before had been rough, communicating anger, dominance, and a kind of frightening awareness of the physical power of the man. But that same power now was simply holding her, sheltering her. The limpness in her mind and body she no longer minded, stopped trying to fight it, curling to the safe haven of his chest.

The mattress suddenly met her back. Vaguely she was aware of his hands tugging at her jeans, shrugging them off her. She was shivering again suddenly, aware of him in a different way. He leaned over her to work at the buttons on her shirt, fumbling with the wet material. Then with exasperation he arched up and pressed a swift kiss on her lips. "You know I'd never hurt you," he murmured. The blouse ripped open, the buttons an effort he was not willing to make. From a long way off she knew she was shivering violently, and then a warm blanket was curled around her, her hair smoothed back with his palm, and another kiss brushed on her lips before he got up from the bed. "I'll get you warm, Tish. I'll be right back."

And he was there again soon, though by the time he curled next to her, snuggling the blanket over both of them, she was asleep, only instincts guiding her to move her body back into the warmth he offered.

Trisha woke once for a drink of water and a second time for a call of nature. She remembered neither, and her first real awakening to reality was reluctant, a shaft of blinding sunlight hot on her sleep-laden eyes. Lazily she turned from it, burrowing back into a pillow, vaguely aware in some gray nether world that every muscle ached, that her body simply craved sleep forever, and that nothing could conceivably feel as good as the coolish soft sheets and downy pillow.

"Tish. Wake up, love. Just to eat. You can go back to sleep, I promise."

"No."

Vaguely she heard the faint velvet chuckle, muffled from where her head had burrowed beneath the pillow. The cocoon of sheet was gradually stolen from her body, and then two palms snuggled at the sides of her neck, smoothing out the muscle cramps that even sleep had not been able to penetrate. Her eyes blinked open into the pillow as the gradual massage took in shoulders and spine, stealing to her sides where just the edge of her breasts were available to his hands. It was such an incredible effort to move, yet she curled just a little so that his hand could massage her breast, what he obviously wanted to do, and then did, kneading a pulsing rhythm into the firm flesh until her sluggish heartbeat changed rhythm...

She groped startling awake then, jerking away with wide eyes to lean back up against the headboard, feeling completely disoriented as she stared warily at Kern.

He'd pulled on an old pair of cutoffs; not bothered

with anything else. He had the nerve to look not only wide awake but rested, the gray look of exhaustion gone and only a faint tinge of shadow remaining beneath his eyes. He radiated an awareness of her and a determination in the way he stood watching her that struck a chord of panic within.

"We're going to spend the day in bed," he drawled lazily. "But it's been more than fifteen hours since either of us has had anything to eat. Now there's a hunger and there's a hunger, Tish, you can choose..."

"Kern..." There was a tray, she saw, on the floor.

"I built a fire for the coffee. There's no power yet. That left bread and canned goods, but the coffee won't stay hot forever. This is a one-shot choice, bright eyes, because just like you, the inclination is to sleep another twelve hours or so."

Hunger suddenly gnawed at her stomach. Avoiding his eyes, she reached to cover herself with the sheet, awkwardly draping it over herself as she stumbled first to the bathroom where she found a pitcher of water. Something else he must have done whenever he had gotten up. The splash of moisture on her face helped, but she groaned when she looked in the mirror, grabbing for a brush. The golden hair was rain-softened and shiny, but hopelessly curly and unmanageable. Without makeup to cover the shadows, her eyes looked huge sapphires. It was just not the way she wanted to look, facing Kern again, with the sheet trailing behind her like a child playing house. She felt defensive and awkward, and it certainly didn't help that she knew she had slept naked, curled to him the entire night.

He was crouched by the tray when she came back in, but he rose as she crossed the room. It was only when she had kneeled down on the carpet beside the tray that she heard the click of the lock behind her. She whirled around in time to see the key buried in the pocket of his cutoffs.

"That's called nowhere to run," he said deliberately.

"I'm not *running* anywhere," she said, snipping back. "I left, Kern; there's a difference."

"The hell there is!"

She drew in her breath when he loomed closer, but he only crouched down again. The feast was peanut butter and jelly sandwiches, a plastic container of berries, luke-warm coffee served in paper cups. Sunlight streamed on all of it as they ate across from each other, the vibrations shooting across the little tray as if it were a magnetic field in a lightning storm, but their appetites were affected not at all. She was starving, so was he; nothing in heaven or hell could have tasted better.

When she was done, she crouched over to take care of the paper plates and empty cups, not looking at him. "I need to go out, Kern," she murmured awkwardly.

"No, you don't."

"Yes, I do. I need to..." She faltered when his eyes finally captured hers. It wasn't really a bathroom she had in mind but the road, but she couldn't look at him and lie. She never had been able to.

"Need to," he repeated gently. "Need to, Tish... what about want to? Tell me what you want to do..."

She shook her head, wishing desperately that the hor-rible, drained sensation would leave her, the weariness of so many days of stress that a few simple hours' sleep simply hadn't cured. "I can't talk about it, Kern. Please..." she pleaded softly.

"*Why* can't you?"

"Because I'll just start crying." A rueful smile trembled on her lips, her sapphire eyes haunted. "You wouldn't be able to hear me then, anyway. Oh, Kern, just leave it—you know it's best..."

The tray slid from between them as he shoved it to a distance. Both his arms lifted in front of him, simply suspended in thin air, waiting. The distance was so short to the cradle of his body; tears were already helplessly falling as he pulled her onto his lap, rocking her like a child, smoothing back her hair. "I couldn't bear it when I found you gone, Tish. I couldn't believe it. I still don't. And when I saw you at camp, looking so dragged-out tired and so beautiful in the rain, I wanted to kill you for risking coming here, for being so close to the fire. If something had happened to you..."

"I had to know you were all right. I had to..." The tears choked in her throat. Her whole body was shuddering, curled into the circle of his arms. "All they'd say on the television was that the fire was west of the Smokies. What else could I do?" The tears finally lessened, and she cupped her palms tightly over her eyes.

"What else could you do?" he repeated dryly, and very gently shifted her to face away from him, his legs cradling both sides of her. Tugging the sheet to her waist, he pressed a kiss in the hollow between her neck and shoulders again. "Since you don't give a hoot in hell, Tish, there wasn't a reason for you to do anything. You left, didn't you?" he whispered. "Put your head down. No, never mind."

His fingers had started to knead her scalp but abruptly changed course. Before she could protest she found the rest of the sheet twisted from her and a bed of white linen made over the plush carpet. "Kern, please don't," she said helplessly. "Please—I don't want this."

"Yes, I know." He untangled her from the tense curl as if she were clay to be remolded, and then he molded. Both his hands worked the length of the back of her right leg, then the left, working out tension, working like a sensual, possessive drug. Kern's touch, the label on the drug, and the addiction she already knew she couldn't fight. "You left the first time because you didn't want this. Then I could understand, Tish. I rushed you into marriage; I rushed you into bed. I wanted to give you the patience you seemed to need so badly, but as soon as I touched you . . . I wanted you so badly. And to see that look of fear in your eyes . . . I know I hurt you, Tish, but I never, never meant to . . ."

A flush like fever warmed her skin as his hands strayed up, kneading at the firm curve of her hips and the base of her spine. Her eyes closed again, urging back tears of a different flavor. She felt, in his touch, in his words, the loving she had been so sure wasn't there. He crouched over her, straddling her thighs as he worked the length of her back, smooth long strokes that vibrated with emotion from his hands.

"And you're going to tell me that you left this time because you didn't want this," he murmured. "That's all it could have been, Tish, because the rest was fine. You know it was. You love the land like I do and you took to the life. So you need more than a house, and there aren't any buyer positions in seven-story department stores, but you'll never convince me that really mattered. You were so happy that day we flew over the land. You took to decorating my mother's room, and you knew you could take on that shop you said you wanted once . . ."

His mouth suddenly followed his hands, his lips caressing the long stretch of soft skin, his arms cradling the sides of her. Her body went silk for him, liquid silk.

A radiant feeling of life was in her flesh and she craved to touch him . . .

"So this time you loved the life, Tish, and that left only us. You care. It showed in your jealousy of Rhea. It showed the morning we talked in my office. And we still share the same dream—you would never have come back and worn yourself out working in that fire otherwise. And I saw you at that waterfall, Tish, before we made love. So that leaves us sex, just like it left us before. You want to tell me that you don't want to be touched— not by me. There just isn't any chemistry, is there. I just leave you neutral . . ."

Kern turned her beneath him, stradling now the front of her thighs. The tenderness in his eyes was touched with despair, a pain she could hardly bare to see, and there was anger in his voice she knew graveled over that pain. "You're lying to yourself, Tish, not to me! I can just look at you—there's need in your eyes right now, desire. Your pulse is racing like white-water rapids; your flesh gives in my hands; your breasts are already swollen and I haven't even touched them . . ."

Gently her fingertips stroked his chest, soothing. "I love you, Kern," she said softly. "I love it when you touch me. I always did. The only reason I left was because I thought you didn't want me!"

He leaned over with his lips parted to say something, but she pressed her fingertip to his mouth to stop him, shaking her head, the barest sheen of moisture in her eyes. "I knew you wanted me—in bed. That didn't mean you wanted me as a wife again, Kern, someone to share your time and your problems and, yes, our old dreams. If you'd asked me here, perhaps I would have read it all differently, but you didn't ask. I was just forced on you because of your mother. So you wanted to make love to me—and, God, I wanted you to—and we did, Kern, and then I asked you. You said you'd never ask me to stay again—"

"I was *trying* to tell you that I said it all when I married you, Tish." Kern almost growled as he leaned over her. "That that was a *commitment* for all time as far as I was concerned, but that I would never, never force or rush you into anything again. The choice had to be yours. I couldn't ever again live with forcing you into something you weren't ready for or didn't want."

"But I thought it had to come from you," she whispered, "because I was the one who failed you before."

His eyes clouded, his palms cupping her face. "Tish, you never failed me in anything," he said softly. "You were just young. I could have done it differently..."

"I never wanted you different and I never blamed you, Kern..." Like the waste of the fire, she felt the waste of so many years without him, so many years she could have loved him, been loved. She wound her arms around his neck and pulled him to her. Fiercely their lips met, an odd trembling in his body that communicated to her own, was matched in her own. If she had finally lost inhibitions with him at the waterfall, it was still nothing like now.

She reached for him in joy, caressing his neck and chest and back. It was all such riches—the way his heartbeat surged beneath her fingertips, the way his body was so beautifully male, his hard-muscled thighs no less arousing than the grainy skin of his tanned neck. A new rhythm kept beating inside, building; she didn't want to give in to it yet. She wanted to savor the sensual sweetness of just freely loving him, and there was no part of him she didn't want to touch, to learn all over again in loving...

He understood so well, loving her body with the same wonder that she loved his. But it was not the same. She could touch so easily, but not be touched so easily— there was a spot in the V of her throat where she could not bear the stroking caress of his lips. Her breasts had swelled before he touched them, but the languid lick of his tongue made her senses feel like velvet. Her back arched for closeness, rhythm inside beginning to sound in her ears, blocking out day and place and sunlight. The brush of his beard in the hollow of her stomach, and— "No more, Kern, please . . ."

Sensations swarmed her senses. His lips covered the pleading in her throat, but he would not give in yet. His palm smoothed its way down her throat and breast and navel, to the silky down between her thighs until the rhythm was the only thing in her bloodstream, a surging love that craved completion.

"I love you, Tish, I love you, I love you . . ."

Her voice echoed the chorus, the song in her heart, the rhythm of passion rich in her blood and in her skin. When he moved over her, she felt his love, his cherishing in every motion he made. He took her with such sweet fierceness that she lost Tish completely, became part of Kern, their limbs and minds inseparable.

"Kern?"

Lazily Kern opened his eyes, inches from her own. They shared the same pillow, lying face-to-face, and Kern's arm was draped over her shoulder. "I keep thinking about the fire," she murmured. "I keep thinking of you close to it, if it had been our land, if . . ."

Gently she was tugged closer, sheltered next to his chest. "It started high, that was the problem," he said quietly. "The sparks shot down, starting dozens of little fires. Anyone who could run, walk, or crawl came to help, Tish, but not to play hero or try to do the firemen's job. The area's been so dry, and more sparks could have fallen. People were working as lookouts, to make sure that when one fire was out it stayed out."

"And that was what you were doing? You weren't any closer than that?"

"Mmmm." His eyes closed again, and Trisha raised up on one elbow, tugging at his beard. His lashes shuttered open again in response, but there was a deliberate effort not to meet her eyes. His gaze fell instead on the bare flesh in front of him. "The beard has to go," he murmured as he raised up to kiss the tender hollow between her breasts. And it was tender, roughed from his love play. "We can't have you bruised, bright eyes . . ."

"You *were* in the thick of it, weren't you?" she asked suspiciously.

"No one was hurt beyond the two in the beginning. Oh, cuts and scrapes, of course. The destruction could have been much worse." He sounded as interested in talking fires as he would have about shuttling to the moon. She shivered all over when one finger stroked the hollow in her throat, and he looked up at her with a wicked smile. "You just can't stand that, can you?" He leaned up to kiss the spot, one, two, three soft kisses, and then arched back, watching the goose bumps with satisfaction. "You've got one or two other little spots that seem to make you forget all about . . ."

"Kern!" Her flush made him chuckle, and she curled closer to him, slowly stroking the flat of his stomach that was just as susceptible to her touch. "I'll find out," she promised, as she nipped tiny bites into his shoulder. "Maybe not from you, Kern. Sooner or later you'll have to unlock that door . . ."

"But not now." He leaned over her, pinning her gently to the pillow, his eyes glinting devil-fire mischief on hers. "We need *rest*. We've both been up for more than two days straight with only a few hours sleep in between."

"Rest," she repeated innocently. "And that's why you insisted on a day in bed, Kern?"

"It certainly is."

"For another minute and a half," she suggested as she ran her fingers gently down the slope of his back, urging him to her with the promise in her eyes.

"For thirty seconds," he amended as his lips came down on hers.

10

FIVE WOMEN WERE gathered in the living room: Trisha and Rhea, a woman named Lotto, who was one of the ranger's wives, and two local women with the soft twang of Tennessee in their speech. The quilting frame had all but temporarily destroyed the living room's decor, but the pattern was nearly done. It was Trisha's design and she called it "night song." The colors in the quilt were the colors of the mountains—vibrant greens and dark browns, the lemon of sun and the clear blue of a summer sky.

The shop Trisha had wanted was more than a possibility. The shop space she'd found to rent was ideal in location, and she'd spent weeks searching out local women who might be interested in selling their wonderful quilts and rugs and needlework. But this one quilt was hers, and the laughter and joy that had already gone into it was reflected in the clear sapphire brightness of her eyes, in the smile that never seemed to leave her these days.

"Patricia!"

Her head jerked up from the needle at the surprising virulence in Kern's tone. Her giant stood in the doorway with the flap of an envelope in his hand, glowering directly at her.

"Would you mind coming here for a moment?"

"Whoops. I'd tread lightly," Rhea whispered teasingly next to her.

Trisha chuckled, divesting herself of threads and needles and patches and chair legs. The smock she wore was pale pink, loose and cool for the late August day, and open to show the creamy smoothness of her throat. Kern was already stalking back to his office, expecting her to follow, which she did, curious, more alert than annoyed at his unusually domineering attitude.

When she entered his quiet study, he pushed at the door behind her, all but slamming it closed. "I got a letter from my mother today," he started out heavily. "Enclosed was a letter for you, which I mistook as a letter for me—" It was all very confusing, until he handed her the sheets of paper. "It evidently followed you all over the city. First to your apartment, then to where you were working, back to your apartment, and finally to my mother's..."

She glanced up with a worried frown at the first line of the letter, studying Kern carefully. Her frown lifted, just a little. It had started out to be a very good act of vibrating anger, but his mouth was twitching. He was not as upset as he was trying to make her believe he was. She scanned the contents of the letter quickly:

"Patricia ... you left so quickly that I didn't have the chance to put these papers together for you ... realized your state of upset ... my professional opinion, to put it in the vernacular, is to take him for all you can get, Patricia ... feel you should reconsider the position you took ... unable to make a decision at that time...I am in the position...sign below; it will give me the authority..."

There was a postcript referring to a potential dinner invitation.

Trisha refolded the papers from Cal Whitaker, slipped them neatly back in the envelope, and tore them in half. The memory of that afternoon in his office whipped through her mind, an agony she thought she'd forgotten, and she looked up at Kern again with troubled eyes.

Kern took the two parts of the envelope from her hands and ripped the rest over and over into little pieces, glaring at her one minute, and the next tossing the whole mess in the air so that it floated down like snow. Her eyes widened, and then he burst out laughing. "So he had a hard time convincing you to go after what was 'rightfully yours,' did he? Tell me about it, Tish," Kern suggested dangerously.

"Kern!" She sidestepped, wanting to laugh with him, as his hand reached for her but grabbed at air. She retreated two more steps as he advanced one more. "I want to tell you," she tried to say gravely. "The day I left here I went to see him and walked out, Kern, I couldn't... and then there was the fire. I heard about it the same night. I would have made sure he understood I didn't want— but I forgot him, Kern, I..."

His damned arms were so long. Behind the desk was no shield. She was caught, and before she could maneuver he had lifted her up and over and they were both sitting in his overstuffed chair in the corner. "I thought you wanted to be free," she said simply, kissing his cheek, his forehead, his eyelids to close down that glowering expression in his eyes. "It wasn't something I ever wanted, Kern, I was trying to do what I thought you—"

"To hell with that. I want to know what he thinks he's doing inviting you out for dinner!"

She chuckled, her fingers reaching teasingly for the buttons on his shirt, her lips brushing apologies on his throat. "Well, he's just got that kind of ego, Kern; that's his problem. You wouldn't have cared anyway, would you have? I mean, you could have written him a legal brief yourself on what a frigid little wife you used to have..."

His mouth pressed on hers, shutting off her teasing, invoking all the promises of loving they knew in each other. "You've burst like a flower, Tish," he murmured softly. "So much love in you—I can't get enough..."

"And I've decided he's right," she murmured back, hiding her face in his neck when his fingers reached beneath the soft pink fabric to play against her skin. His fingers stilled.

"I beg your pardon?"

"He's right," she repeated teasingly, her eyes wide open and innocent on his as she escaped from his lap before he could catch her again. "I have every intention of 'taking you for all I can get,' Kern. Although I certainly don't have money in mind!"

"You come back here!"

She shook her head with a radiant smile. "I've got a houseful of people," she said scolding. "But Kern...when I went into town this morning..." She hesitated and then opened the door. "You know that little creek, about a twenty-minute walk from the camp? I think we should do the next one there. And for the third baby, we could go back to the waterfall again..."

"Trisha!"

She closed the door, singing with mischief and laughter and love inside. The four women were waiting with raised heads, demanding to know what Kern had wanted, teasing her for the flush of pink on her cheeks as she settled down to work again. The quilt was within an hour of being done. The women would go then. She could wait, to really savor the news with Kern. The look on his face had told her all she needed to know, that first startled expression rapidly changing to elation. He wanted children. Her children. And she felt absolutely exhilarated.

Kern was suddenly a giant in the doorway again, silent this time, his eyes strictly on his wife. The four other women glanced up at him and then at each other.

"It's not as though we can't finish this another time," Rhea said as she moved toward the door.

"Yes," Trisha said helplessly.

In five minutes they were alone in the room. "You didn't really expect to just drop fireworks like that—" Kern started vibrantly.

"No." She shook her head, laughing as she crossed the room to him. "I meant to tell you after a terrific dinner with chilled champagne. But I couldn't wait, Kern." She wound her arms around his neck, looking up at him with love-filled eyes. "I love you so!"

"And I love you," he murmured deeply, and dipped his head to kiss her. "How soon?" he whispered.

"March," she whispered back.

"You need *rest*," he scolded, as his lips gently claimed hers over and over.

"Rest?" She reminded him teasingly as she felt his fingers unsnapping the back of her dress. His hand faltered.

"Tish, if you actually need—"

She shook her head. "What I need, Kern, is you." Fleetingly she thought how good and easy it was to say those words. And as Kern removed the last of their clothing, a look of happiness and love on his face, Trisha welcomed him with open arms, certain they shared the joy of knowing they were building a rich, new life— together.

WATCH FOR
6 NEW TITLES EVERY MONTH!

Second Chance at Love

WHAT READERS SAY ABOUT
SECOND CHANCE AT LOVE BOOKS

"Your books are the greatest!"
—*M. N., Carteret, New Jersey**

"I have been reading romance novels for quite some time, but the SECOND CHANCE AT LOVE books are the most enjoyable."
—*P. R., Vicksburg, Mississippi**

"I enjoy SECOND CHANCE [AT LOVE] more than any books that I have read and I do read a lot."
—*J. R., Gretna, Louisiana**

"I really think your books are exceptional . . . I read Harlequin and Silhouette and although I still like them, I'll buy your books over theirs. SECOND CHANCE [AT LOVE] is more interesting and holds your attention and imagination with a better story line . . ."
—*J. W., Flagstaff, Arizona**

"I've read many romances, but yours take the 'cake'!"
—*D. H., Bloomsburg, Pennsylvania**

"Have waited ten years for *good* romance books. Now I have them."
—*M. P., Jacksonville, Florida**

*Names and addresses available upon request